Praise for

I0617706

Brookside Athletic Club

Ms. Lynne creates some of the strongest characters and heartfelt stories I have ever read. I'll Stand By You is a great addition to her library. ~ *Dark Divas Reviews*

The concept works, the story flows well and once the plot focuses more on Ray and Mike, it moves faster. Their attraction is strong initially, got more so as the story progresses and once it turns physical, it is sizzling hot. These two have a lot in common and the author did a nice job expressing how well they related to each other… ~ *Literary Nymphs Reviews*

The sex is hot and varied, and the characters draw the reader into their stories… A good read. ~ *Love Romances*

'I'll Stand By You' is the perfect title for this inspirational love story and as I read, I heard the song by the same name playing in the background saying "I'll stand by you, I won't let anyone hurt you, I'll stand by you." It's a reminder for us to strive to give those we love the unconditional love all of us deserve, but only a lucky few of us receive. I recommend this book to anyone with a romantic heart, who enjoys a story where love prevails over selfishness and despair. Thanks, Carol, for another heartwarming story. I'm looking forward to more great books in this new series. ~ *QMO Books*

Total-E-Bound Publishing books by Carol Lynne:

Campus Cravings Volume One: On the Field
Coach
Side-Lined

Sacking the Quarterback

Campus Cravings Volume Two: Off the Field
Off Season
Forbidden Freshman

Campus Cravings Volume Three: Back on Campus
Broken Pottery
In Bear's Bed

Campus Cravings Volume Four: Dorm Life
Office Advances
A Biker's Vow

Campus Cravings Volume Five: BK House
Hershie's Kiss
Theron's Return

Campus Cravings Volume Six
Incoming Freshman
A Lesson Learned

Campus Cravings
Live for Today

Campus Cravings Volume Seven
Locky in Love
The Injustice of Being

Campus Cravings
Watch Me

Good-Time Boys
Sonny's Salvation
Garron's Gift

Rawley's Redemption
Twin Temptations
It's a Good Life

Cattle Valley Volume One
All Play & No Work
Cattle Valley Mistletoe

Cattle Valley Volume Two
Sweet Topping
Rough Ride

Cattle Valley Volume Three
Physical Therapy
Out of the Shadow

Cattle Valley Volume Four
Bad Boy Cowboy
The Sound of White

Cattle Valley Volume Five
Gone Surfin'
The Last Bouquet

Cattle Valley Volume Six
Eye of the Beholder
Cattle Valley Days

Cattle Valley Volume Seven
Bent— Not Broken
Arm Candy

Cattle Valley Volume Eight
Recipe for Love
Firehouse Heat

Cattle Valley Volume Nine
Neil's Guardian Angel
Scarred

Seasons of Love Volume One
Spring

Seasons of Love Volume Two
Summer
Fall

Seasons of Love Volume Three
Winter

Neo's Realm Vol 1
Liquid Crimson
Blood Trinity

Neo's Realm
Crimson Moon

Anthologies
Legend: Healing Doctor Ryan
Stealing My Heart: Stolen Memories
Fabulous Brits: Moor Love
Nuahgty Nooners: Dalton's Awakening
Gaymes: Highland Gaymes
Unconventional at Best: A New Normal

Karaoke at the Tumbleweed
Joey's First Time
Between Two Lovers
Corporate Passion
Reunion
Sunset Ridge
Broken Colour
Dead Man Living

BROOKSIDE ATHLETIC CLUB
CLUB
Volume One

I'll Stand By You

Soul Restoration

CAROL LYNNE

Brookside Athletic Club Volume One
ISBN # 978-1-78184-606-3
©Copyright Carol Lynne 2013
Cover Art by Posh Gosh ©Copyright 2013
Interior text design by Claire Siemaszkiewicz
Total-E-Bound Publishing

Published in 2013 by Total-E-Bound Publishing, Think Tank, Ruston Way, Lincoln, LN6 7FL, United Kingdom.

.

I'LL STAND BY YOU

Dedication

I have always considered The Pretenders song, I'll
Stand by You, an anthem to unconditional love. Mike,
from this story, was first introduced in the Seasons of
Love series as a minor character. I intended him to
stay a secondary character, but he stole a piece of my
heart, and I knew I couldn't close that series without
giving Mike the soulmate he so
desperately longed for.

Chapter One

Arriving in Kansas City after a long drive from Chicago, Mike Shriver pulled into his clients' driveway. Ray DeMonico and Brent Atwood obviously had excellent taste, and by the look of the house, a hefty bank account. The large Tudor-style home was exactly as he'd pictured it after talking to Ray for hours over the phone. He'd met the two men only once, when he'd flown in to take final measurements and contract a foundation company.

The meeting with Ray and Brent had gone well, and when a room was offered in the couple's home for the duration of the job, Mike had taken them up on it. He got out of his pickup and opened the back driver's side door. The backseat was full of tools, blueprints and anything else he could think of that he'd need for the projected eight month schedule.

"Need help?" an enthusiastic sounding voice asked.

Mike glanced over his shoulder at Brent. "Sure." He handed Brent the rolls of blueprints he wanted to go over with the two men. "If you can get these, I'll grab my suitcases. Is this a secure enough area to lock my tools up and leave 'em out here?"

"Probably, but Ray cleared a bay in the garage for you just in case. If you want to pull around, he's already got the door open for you."

"Sounds good." Mike shut the back door and climbed behind the wheel as Brent disappeared into the house. It was hard to believe the two had not only invited him into their home for the better part of a year, but had made room for his work truck. He slowly pulled into the garage, praying the long extended-cab would fit.

Ray opened the door that led into the house and held up his hands to indicate Mike still had another foot of room. Mike nodded his thanks and put the truck in park. Before getting out, he took a moment to stare at Ray through his mirrored sunglasses. Although both men were hot, Mike and Ray had connected with each other almost immediately. Despite feeling guilty about it, Mike looked his fill before getting out of the truck. "Thanks for the space."

"No problem. We use this bay for storage more than anything."

Brent stepped into the garage and wrapped an arm around Ray's waist. "I hope you're hungry. Ray's been cooking all afternoon."

"Starved," Mike said, squeezing between the front bumper and the wall with his suitcases in hand. "I thought about stopping in Des Moines, but wasn't sure what the two of you had planned, so I decided against it."

Ray took one of Mike's suitcases and led the way into the house.

Mike was so focused on the fantastic smells wafting from the stove; he didn't immediately notice Brent standing behind him. When a hand landed on his ass, Mike jumped in surprise.

"I'm glad you're here," Brent said, winking.

Mike's immediate reaction was to look at Ray who was shaking his head with a resigned expression on his face.

"Sorry," Ray said. "Brent doesn't always know when to behave himself."

"Don't apologise for me." Brent released Mike's ass and hopped up onto the black granite kitchen island. "I know a good ass when I see one. I was just confirming my suspicions."

Mike took off his sunglasses and set them on the counter. He wasn't sure if he should comment or not. Ray didn't seem angry at Brent, but he did sound embarrassed by his partner's actions.

"As far as rooms, you've got your pick. We have four guest rooms or, something I thought would be even better, a studio apartment over the garage. It's supposed to be for hired help, but with only the two of us here, we don't need anything but a weekly spit and shine," Ray said, moving to the stove to stir the sauce.

"The studio sounds good. That way I won't have to be in your hair any more than necessary," Mike replied.

Bracing his hands on the edge of the island, Brent leant forward. "The room across the hall from ours is a lot nicer."

Ray hit the wooden spoon on the edge of the pot harder than necessary before he set it down. "I'll help you take your things up to the studio."

Mike wasn't sure what was going on between the two men, but he nodded and picked up his suitcase. He followed Ray up the staircase just off the kitchen and took the opportunity to check out the man's ass. The first time they'd met, Ray had worn a suit. Mike had to admit Ray's ass was better displayed in the pair of worn jeans he currently wore.

The staircase opened up into a large room with a small kitchenette in one corner, a bed in the far corner as well as an enclosed space Mike assumed was the bathroom. The centre of the room held worn, but nice, leather furniture. "This is fantastic."

"Thanks. We recently redid the family room, so I had them put all the old furniture up here. Well, except the bed, that came from my bachelor days." Ray chuckled as he carried Mike's suitcase towards the bed. "If that bed could talk I'd be in a world of trouble."

The statement caused Mike's cock to perk up. He set the second suitcase down. "Are you sure about this?"

"I'm sure."

"Let me know if I start to wear out my welcome, and I'll find a hotel or something," Mike said.

"Brent made you nervous, didn't he?" Ray asked.

Nervous wasn't exactly the word Mike would have used. "Is there something going on I should know about?"

Ray leant back against the antique wardrobe. "Around three years ago, Brent decided he wanted to try a threesome. It wasn't something I was interested in, but I went along with it because I was afraid of losing him." He took a deep breath and crossed his arms over his chest. "Since then we've done it a few times, but never for more than a weekend. When I told him I'd invited you to stay here while the athletic club is built, he just assumed you'd spend some time in our bed. I tried to tell him it wouldn't work because you weren't some random stranger we could just get rid of after the weekend, but Brent argued that you were an adult and could make up your own mind."

Mike scratched his jaw. He'd slept with more than one guy before but only once and he'd been really drunk at the time. Still… "I won't lie and tell you the idea doesn't intrigue me, but my brothers would kick my ass if I did anything to screw up this job."

Ray nodded. "That's exactly what I told Brent."

Mike tried to wrap his mind around the situation. "Doesn't it bother you to see him fucking someone else?"

"It nearly killed me at first, but then I realised how much he'd given up to be with me, and I knew it wouldn't be fair to him to say no."

"Bullshit," Mike said, thinking of his dear friend Sidney. "When you love someone, there's nothing wrong with wanting them all to yourself." He'd never planned to fall in love with Sidney, but it had been hard to resist the hot little architect who worked for his brother. Even knowing Sidney was deeply committed to his partner, Nash, hadn't been enough to stop Mike from falling head-over-heels for him. It was the foremost reason Mike had agreed to relocate to Kansas City until the health club was complete.

"I understand what you're saying, but I think sometimes you can love someone so much you'd do just about anything to make them happy," Ray countered.

"And does it?"

Ray nodded. "Yeah. Brent's a completely different person for a while after we do it."

"Different how?" Mike asked.

"Happier. He hangs on my every word and feels the desire to touch me whenever we're in the same room together." Ray grinned, showing off twin dimples.

"It's nice to feel wanted like that again. Maybe he was right, maybe things were starting to get a little stale."

"So you're okay with it now?" Mike was definitely interested in going a few rounds, but the whole situation still worried him.

"Yeah, I guess so. I mean, I've seen that it only makes things better between us. And, it's nice to feel taken care of once in a while. It seems I'm always the one to top, but there are times I miss the feel of a dick in my ass." Ray bit his bottom lip. Although Mike doubted Ray meant it sexually, the simple gesture tested Mike's willpower.

"The most important thing to me is keeping my relationship with Brent safe." Ray pushed away from the wardrobe and ran his hand across the front of his tented pants. "I'd better get downstairs or my sauce'll burn. Dinner should be on the table in thirty minutes if you want to shower or anything first."

"Thanks." Mike watched Ray disappear down the steps before sitting on the corner of the bed. "Wow."

* * * *

Ray gave his sauce a quick stir before turning on the flame under the pasta pot. Once he was satisfied the sauce wouldn't burn, he went in search of Brent. "Hey," he said, finding Brent sprawled out on the sofa in front of the television. "You didn't even give Mike a chance to unpack before making him uncomfortable."

"I couldn't help myself." Brent snuggled his way into Ray's arms. "One look at those big muscles in that tight T-shirt he was wearing and I almost tripped over my tongue."

"I agree that he's pretty damn incredible looking, but this is an entirely different situation than we've ever put ourselves in. We need Mike to head up this construction project. The last thing we can afford is to piss off our contractor before he even gets started."

"So you're telling me he'll be here for months, and I'm not allowed to touch him?" Brent gave Ray a quick kiss, using only the tip of his tongue to tease. "I'm not sure I can do that."

"Well you're going to have to try unless Mike makes the first move." Ray silently prayed that Mike would make a move. It was the first time since he'd agreed to indulge in the occasional threesome that he really wanted another man besides Brent. He gazed into Brent's sapphire blue eyes. "If Mike's okay with it, I'm okay with it, but it needs to be his decision. Got it?"

Brent licked his lips. "Can I tease him until he gives in?"

"Make him uncomfortable and I'll kick your ass," Ray warned.

"You mean you'll kiss my ass," Brent countered.

Ray had often wondered what his life would've been like if Brent had never wandered into his lecture hall and caught his attention. If the affair between them had never been exposed, and Ray hadn't been fired, would they still be together or would their relationship have already fizzled out on its own? The fact that Brent had quit college to follow Ray back to his hometown of Kansas City was another thing Ray often considered, because although Ray had already loved Brent, he hadn't felt responsible for Brent until he'd given up everything to be with him.

"Where'd you go?" Brent asked, moving to straddle Ray's lap.

"Just thinking." Ray squeezed Brent's ass. "Have you talked to your parents lately?"

"Yesterday," Brent said, grinding his erection against Ray. "Mom sends her love."

"But Dad didn't, right?" Ray ran his fingers up and down the seam of Brent's jeans. There was definitely no love lost between Ray and Brent's father. Brock believed Ray had taken advantage of Brent's youth and led his son astray, while Ray had come to realise that Brent had a bit of a daddy fetish and had always gone after older men without his father's knowledge.

"Forget about my father and fuck me."

Ray was incredibly tempted. It had been a while since the two of them had enjoyed spontaneous sex, but they had a guest in the house. "I'd love to, but I told Mike to come down for dinner after he showered."

"And he did," Mike said from the doorway. "Sorry to interrupt."

Ray removed his hands from Brent's ass. "Would you do me a favour and stir the sauce? I'll be in shortly."

"Sure."

After Mike left, Ray pulled Brent's head down for a kiss. The kiss started hot and progressed until it was a blending of tongue and teeth and raw need. What Ray wouldn't give to strip Brent out of his jeans and fuck him right there over the sofa, but he knew half of the passion he felt was a direct result of Mike walking in on them. He pulled back and smiled at Brent as he wiped his chin. "Later."

"For you maybe. I'm gonna go into the bedroom and finish myself off," Brent said, standing. He pulled Ray to his feet and palmed the front of his jeans. "You sure you don't want to join me?"

"Dinner's waiting," Ray reminded Brent, grinding his cock against Brent's. He left Brent and walked through the formal dining room on his way to the kitchen. Before entering, he took a couple of deep breaths, trying to get his cock under control. "Sorry about that," he said, joining Mike at the stove.

"Your house," Mike reminded.

Ray uncovered the homemade pasta he'd made earlier in the day. "I hope you like spaghetti." He picked up the angel hair pasta and gently dropped it into the boiling water.

"You bet. Although I'm not sure I've ever had anyone make it from scratch like this." Mike lowered the flame under the sauce and set the spoon to the side. "Where'd you learn to do this?"

"My Grandma DeMonico insisted all her grandchildren learn how to make the family recipes before she died, although she called sauce gravy."

Mike bumped his hip against Ray's. "Now I have even more reason to be jealous."

Ray lifted the pot and poured the pasta into a strainer. "What else are you jealous of? You want Brent?"

Mike sighed and turned to face Ray. "Yeah, I think I do. Seeing the two of you earlier must've melted my brain."

Ray shook the pasta several times before pouring it onto a large platter he already had sitting out. "You have someone special back in Chicago, Mike?"

Mike closed his eyes and rubbed his forehead. "There's someone very special in Chicago, unfortunately, he's in love with someone else."

"Ouch, that sucks." Ray carried the platter to the stove. He removed a ladle from the large utensil carafe and used it to spoon sauce over the pasta. "Did you have an affair with him?" he asked out of curiosity.

"No. Sidney's hopelessly devoted to Nash."

Ray was surprised to hear his architect's name. "I've met them. They're both nice guys."

"Yeah, that's the part that sucks."

Ray opened the warming oven and removed the meatballs he'd prepared earlier and spooned them onto the platter on top of the pasta and sauce. "So, is there anyone besides Sidney?" He silently prayed the answer would be no.

"Nope, at least not anyone I see on a regular basis."

Ray's biggest fear had always been Brent leaving him for one of their occasional lovers. "If anything happens between you and Brent or whatever, I need you to promise you won't fall in love and try to take him away from me."

"I tried for five years to fall in love with another man, and I couldn't. I can't tell you how hard I've tried to get Sidney out of my heart, but it simply isn't possible."

Ray noticed Mike didn't deny the idea of getting together with Brent, but at least he'd feel better if he did. "Brent will try to torture you until he gets his way. If you're not into it, just tell him, and he'll back off eventually."

"What about you?" Mike asked, moving closer to Ray.

"What about me?" Ray set the food on the table.

"Are you open to the idea?"

Ray turned to face Mike, less than a foot separating them. "I've thought of little else since the first time I met you."

Mike leaned in for the softest kiss Ray had ever experienced. He wasn't even sure if their lips had actually touched, but it was enough to harden his cock once again. Ray sighed. "You're killing me."

"You're doing the same to me," Mike replied, resting his hand on the small of Ray's lower back. "I know I should back away and give myself time to really think about this, but that's the last thing I want right now."

Ray closed the distance between them, feeling the proof of Mike's desire rub against him. "We'd better eat before everything gets cold. We have the rest of the evening to work out details."

Mike moved, grinding their groins against each other. "As long as the details include getting to know you and Brent better."

Ray smiled. "Definitely." As much as he wanted to kiss Mike again, Ray decided it would be better to wait because he knew once he got started no way in hell would he want to stop. He took a step back, breaking away from Mike and cupped his hands around his mouth. "Brent, dinner," he called.

Mike appeared deep in thought as he sat down and placed a napkin in his lap. "Can I be honest?"

"I wouldn't expect anything less." Ray poured wine into Mike's glass.

"I'm sexually attracted to Brent. Hell, I'd have to be blind not to be. But I *like* you. I enjoy talking to you, being around you..." Mike leaned towards Ray. "Looking at you. I'm not worried about getting too close to Brent to walk away. I worry about leaving you if this goes further."

Ray felt the words like a physical touch. Brent's arrival saved him from commenting and for that, he was grateful. "Food's getting cold."

Brent plopped down in his chair. "Yeah, but it was worth it. Damn, that felt good." He smiled at Mike. "You enjoy jerking off?"

Mike took a sip of wine while maintaining eye contact with Brent.

Ray watched the moment between the two men with growing interest. What did Mike see when he looked at Brent? Did he think Ray was a fool for practically offering Brent up on a silver platter?

"Masturbation has its uses, but when you have someone who loves you, willing to do it for you, what's the point? If I had that, I'd never take myself in hand again," Mike whispered.

Ray squeezed his legs together, trying to alleviate the ache in his groin. He was surprised by the feelings of jealousy that raced through him as Mike spoke of his unrequited love for Sidney.

Brent stood and leaned over the table towards Mike. "And sometimes it's fun to have a totally different hand touch your cock."

"We'll see," Mike whispered in return.

Chapter Two

All through dinner, Mike couldn't take his eyes off the two men across from him. What was it about Brent and Ray that had him ready to jump into bed with them, knowing he'd probably get hurt before his time in Kansas City was over?

"Have you ever watched two guys fuck in front of you, Mike?" Brent asked before taking a drink of wine.

"Yes," Mike answered truthfully. "But I didn't have to worry about seeing them the next day."

Brent refilled his glass, shaking the last drops of wine from the bottle. He scooted his chair back and stood. "What's wrong, you think you won't like us tomorrow if we suck your dick tonight?" He pulled another bottle out of the rack and grabbed the opener from the island.

Mike spread his legs, giving his cock room to harden. "It's not a matter of liking you in the morning; it's whether or not we can still work together if something goes wrong."

Brent, damn him, walked over to stand beside Mike, his arousal on full display. Without a word, Brent squeezed between Mike and the table and straddled Mike's lap. God help him, Mike was mesmerised by Brent's lithe, hard body. "What're you doing?" Mike asked.

Brent draped his arms over Mike's shoulders and swivelled his hips, rubbing his ass against Mike's erection. "Serving you dessert." He leaned in and sealed their lips together, thrusting his tongue deep into Mike's mouth.

With a moan, Mike wrapped his arms around Brent, taking control of the kiss. It had been too long since he'd held a man in his arms. *Too long* since he'd been able to get Sidney off his mind long enough to indulge in hot sex without fear of losing his erection halfway through. He broke the kiss and stared into Brent's big blue eyes before turning to glance at Ray. The longing in Ray's gaze reminded Mike of himself each time he saw Sidney and Nash sharing an intimate moment. His concerns about getting into a sexual relationship with the two men returned full force, causing him to scoot his chair back and help Brent to his feet. "Thank you for the kiss and the fantastic dinner, but I think it would be better if I go up to my room now."

"You can't go yet, we're just getting started," Brent whined, trying to pull Mike towards the living room.

Mike planted his feet and refused to budge. "Stop it," he warned Brent. He yanked his hand free of Brent's grasp and escaped through the door that would take him to his room.

* * * *

The door to the garage apartment slammed shut and Ray braced himself for Brent's temper. He wasn't sure what had gone wrong, but from the narrow-eyed stare he was getting from Brent, it was his fault.

"I hope you're happy with yourself."

"Of course I'm not happy, but I don't know what I did," Ray tried to explain.

"Isn't it obvious?" Brent opened the small coat closet beside the door leading to the garage and removed a jacket. "Once again you've managed to ruin it for me."

Ray stood and took a step towards Brent. "Please don't say that. I wanted him as much as you did."

"Maybe so, but evidently he doesn't want you. So, because of *you*, I don't get to have my fun. That's bullshit, and we both know it." Brent stopped abruptly and shook his head. "I love you, babe, but we both know you're boring, and bringing in a third is the only way we're going to spice up our relationship enough to make it last. So you have a choice, you can either fix this or deal with the consequences."

Ray was stunned. "Are you threatening me?"

Brent opened the door. "No, I'm warning you."

Before Ray could question Brent further he was out the door, leaving Ray shaken. He heard Brent's car roar to life and pull out of the garage bay. Ray took a deep breath and tried to figure out what had gone wrong. It had taken every ounce of willpower to remain seated while Mike explored Brent's mouth with his tongue. For a few blissful moments, Ray had hoped he'd also get the chance to be on the receiving end of Mike's passion, but one glance at Ray and Mike had quickly changed his mind about everything. *Shit.*

Ray reached for his plate and stacked it on top of Brent's. As he carried the dirty dishes to the sink, he tried to think of a way to fix the mess he'd made. He spied his phone on the island and snatched it up before he could change his mind.

"Yeah," Mike answered after several rings.

"Can I come up? I need to talk to you." Ray returned to the table for another load of dishes.

"Why'd Brent leave?"

"That's one of the things I need to speak to you about. I won't pressure you, I just need to talk."

Mike was quiet for several moments before answering. "Sure, come on up."

"Thanks." Ray opened the apartment door and ended the call. There was no doubt in his mind that he was the biggest fool in the world for what he was about to do, but for the first time in his life, he had a home, and he'd do anything to protect it.

Mike was on the sofa with a glass in his hand and a bottle of whisky on the table in front of him.

Ray hovered next to the couch until Mike gestured for him to have a seat. "I'm sorry," Ray began.

"You have nothing to apologise for. I'm the one who ran out of the room with my tail between my legs." Mike tipped the glass back and swallowed some of the dark amber alcohol. "So tell me what's going on with Brent."

Ray settled in the corner of the soft leather sofa. "He blames me." He shrugged, not sure what else to say.

Mike finished his drink before setting the glass on the table. "In a way, I guess I do, too."

Ray rubbed the back of his neck, building the courage to say what he'd come up to say. "You can take me out of the equation if you need to."

"Excuse me?" Mike rested his forearms on his knees, his upper body leaning towards Ray.

"If you want to only fuck Brent, I won't stand in your way."

Mike jumped to his feet and began to pace the room. "What the hell kind of relationship do the two of you have?" He spun around and stared at Ray. "Seriously? You're just going to offer up the man you love for a couple nights of sex?"

Ray's emotions threatened to bubble to the surface. He wasn't the kind of man who cried, so dammit, why did he feel like that's all he wanted to do at the moment. "You'll be the first, but it's obvious the two of you have a connection, and believe me, Brent won't just let it go."

Mike stalked over and pulled Ray to his feet. With his hands on Ray's shoulders, Mike gave him a firm shake. "The reason I couldn't go through with it was because of you, but not for the reasons you seem to think."

In an instant, Mike's hold went from threatening to gentle. He slid his arms around Ray and held him close. "I saw something of myself in your expression after that kiss with Brent and it scared me."

"What did you see?" Ray had tried so hard to mask his thoughts from Mike and Brent, but it was becoming increasingly obvious he'd failed.

"The way you looked at me is the same way I look at Sidney." Mike held Ray even tighter. "I can't do this because I will never fall in love with Brent, but you're a different story. You're exactly the kind of man who could drive my stupid fucking obsession with Sidney away, but where would that leave us? Instead of being in love with Sidney, I'd be in love with you, and just like Sidney, you already belong to someone."

"I'm liking Sidney less and less all the time," Ray mumbled, closing his eyes. It felt so good to be held in Mike's arms that Ray started to question his loyalty to Brent. Sure he'd spent hours getting to know Mike over the phone, but he'd been with Brent for years. "What's wrong with me? I used to be the toughest little bastard on the street, had to be to survive. Now look at me, offering my partner like he was a piece of candy to dangle in front of you just to keep you close to me."

"I think Brent did most of the dangling, so don't carry that guilt. The question I have is why would you let Brent and I fuck just to keep me around?"

"That's not the only reason." Ray never talked about his past, preferring to build a future instead. "I have a real home for the first time in my life. I know Brent gets bored sticking around the house all the time, but for the most part, he does it because he knows how much I love the stability that comes with being in a relationship."

Mike ran his hands up and down Ray's back. "So what does that have to do with me?"

Although Ray knew Mike deserved the truth, it wasn't in him to give it, not about Brent, not yet, so he offered an alternative. "Brent has set his sights on you, and if he doesn't get what he wants, he'll leave me. He told me as much downstairs after you left the table."

Mike took a step back and led Ray to the sofa. "Did you ever stop to think that maybe that would be for the best? It's wrong for him to put you in this position, but he does it because you let him."

Ray nodded. He knew he should be ashamed of the way he let Brent treat him, but it was no different from the way his dad had treated his mom and they were still together. His breath caught in his chest at the comparison. How had he managed to recreate the home he'd fought so hard to get away from? Standing, Ray eased towards the staircase. "I should go. I'll see you in the morning."

Ray left the apartment mortified by the kind of life he'd been living to make Brent happy. How many times had he silently cursed his mom for putting up with a man like his father just to keep peace in the house?

He immediately started to clean the kitchen, a job that had always fallen to him. Ray paused in the process of scraping the left over sauce into a storage container. "What the hell am I doing?"

With a grunt of resignation, Ray finished with the sauce and stuck the container in the freezer. He grinned as he left the dirty pan on the island and walked out of the kitchen, grabbing the bottle of wine and his glass on the way. Let Brent come home to the mess, Ray no longer cared.

* * * *

After four nights of little sleep, Mike was sipping his morning coffee and talking to Sidney on the phone. The forms for the foundation had been completed the day before and the cement truck was scheduled to arrive at eight.

"You added the extra footings under the waterfall, right?" Sidney was a perfectionist. It didn't matter how many times Mike assured his friend he would make the needed adjustments to the blueprints, Sidney continued to worry.

"Yep."

When Ray walked into the kitchen, Mike smiled. "Morning."

"Good morning."

"Ray?" Sidney asked.

"Mmm hmm." Mike tried to keep his mind on the conversation with Sidney, but Ray's worried expression captured his attention. He'd done his best to stay out of the ongoing arguments he'd overheard between Ray and Brent over the last several days, but he couldn't bring himself to ignore Ray's obvious distress. "I'll call you if we run into any problems."

"He's sexy, huh?"

Sidney's question surprised Mike. "Something like that." He averted his gaze when Ray carried his coffee to the table.

"Too bad he's already taken or you could make your time there a lot easier." Sidney chuckled. "I'll let you go. Talk to you later."

"How's Nash?" Not that Mike really cared, but he needed the reminder of why he wasn't supposed to love Sidney.

"Fine. He started working at the garage again part-time. Hopefully it'll pull him out of the funk he's been in lately."

"I hope so. I'll call ya if I need you." Mike hung up and set the phone beside him. He'd only been in Kansas City for five days, but he thought he knew Ray enough to know that something was bothering him. Had Brent gone out again? "Rough night?"

Ray took a sip of his coffee. "I've had better," he mumbled.

"Anything I can do?" Thus far, Mike had thwarted Brent's attempts of seduction and there had been quite a few.

Ray stood and retrieved the coffee pot, bringing it over to the table to refill Mike's cup and top off his own. "Brent still thinks it's my fault you haven't taken him up on his offers."

The statement didn't surprise Mike because Brent had said something similar the day before. Looking into Ray's dark brown eyes, Mike knew he couldn't lie to the man. Ray had been nothing but honest with Mike since he'd arrived and he deserved the same respect. Ray was just as sexy, if not more so, than Brent. Mike leant forward until Ray glanced up from his cup and met his gaze. "After what happened the other night, Brent means absolutely nothing to me. You're the one I can't seem to get off my mind."

"I like having you here." Ray reached out and brushed his fingers across Mike's hand. "I talked to Brent after he stormed out your first night here, and although he was angry at first, he promised that he'd try to ease up on you."

"It's not working," Mike stated the obvious.

"I know, but I'm not willing to give up on everything we've worked so hard to build." Ray took a sip of his coffee. "It's easier for me with you here. I love Brent, I really do, but it's nice to have someone to talk to about what's going on in the world. Brent and I have never really connected on an intellectual level. Maybe it's the age difference, or the fact that we didn't really know each other outside the bedroom before he followed me here, but every time I try to talk about politics or sports, he listens, but he never gets involved in the conversation."

"Why didn't you wake me?" Brent came into the room in nothing but a small pair of bikini boy shorts, his morning erection still on display. He stood beside Ray, but stared at Mike.

"Because you told me last night you weren't interested in watching cement dry." Ray scooted his chair back to make room for Brent.

Brent sat on Ray's lap and reached for Ray's cup. "I changed my mind." He took a drink before giving Ray a deep kiss.

Mike watched the two men closely. Ray's eyelids drifted shut as the kiss intensified while Brent watched Mike out of the corner of his eyes. It was obvious Ray believed they were making up for their earlier argument and Brent was doing everything he could to tease Mike. The two men were so different. Mike had a hard time figuring out how they had lasted so long as a couple. "If you're going with us, you'd better get dressed. The truck'll be on site in less than thirty minutes and it's a fifteen minute drive."

Ray broke the kiss and glanced at the clock. "Shit." He slapped Brent's hip. "Better get moving."

Brent climbed off Ray's lap and made a show of running a hand across his chest, directing Mike's attention to his twin hard nipples. "Any volunteers to help me wash my back?"

Ray smiled up at Brent. "No time. I'll take a rain check."

Brent ran his fingers through Ray's short dark brown hair as he returned his attention to Mike. "Will you give me a rain check, too?"

Mike didn't intend to answer Brent's question. What he really wanted was to slap Brent's hands off Ray's body. *Shit, I'm jealous.*

Brent laughed and left the room.

Ray stood and carried his cup to the sink.

Mike finished his coffee before doing the same. He stood beside Ray, unsure of his next move. Would kissing Ray without Brent in the room be wrong? Deciding to test the waters, Mike put his hand on Ray's shoulder.

It didn't take Ray long to react. He tilted his chin up and brushed his lips across Mike's. "I've wanted to do that for days."

Mike turned to face Ray. "I don't know why I'm doing this, but, God, I want to kiss you." He captured Ray's lips with his, taking the time to gently lead Ray's tongue deep into his mouth. Ray moaned and pressed fully into Mike's arms as the kiss became a carnal need. Mike grabbed Ray's ass and ground against him, trying to relieve the ache in his cock.

"Uhhh." Ray groaned and broke the kiss. "I can't do this without Brent."

Mike reached between them and palmed Ray's erection through his jeans. He was glad to know he wasn't the only one affected by the kiss, but it didn't solve their problem. He refused to fuck Brent just to get to Ray, but at the same time, his nightly dreams of holding Ray were starting to get the better of him.

Mike had argued back and forth with himself many times over the situation. Although Ray was in a relationship like Sidney, Mike didn't consider Brent a third of the man Nash was. Maybe that was the crux of his dilemma. Was it wrong to try to steal Ray away from someone who didn't deserve him? Damn his morals. Mike released Ray and took a step back. "I shouldn't have done that."

"You're probably right." Ray washed the coffee cups and set them beside the sink to dry. "It's not really right for me to tell Brent to lay off when I can't seem to."

"I wish you didn't have to," Mike admitted. "But I don't want Brent, and I'm not sure how I feel about going behind his back."

"I understand."

Mike took a deep breath. The situation with Sidney was screwed up, he was the first to admit it, but his love was real. Unfortunately, if he ever hoped to be happy he needed to make some changes in his life. Sitting around alone every night waiting for a good man like Grady Nash to die just to make his dream of being able to openly love Nash's husband wasn't cool. As a matter of fact, it was embarrassing, pathetic and downright despicable. Mike knew he had to break away from Sidney, but getting into a relationship with Ray when he was still emotionally and sexually tied to Brent wasn't the way to do it. "If only you were single."

Ray filled two travel mugs with coffee before shutting off the pot. "If I was single I wouldn't be able to afford the athletic club which would mean we would've never met."

"Ready." Brent came into the kitchen with his hair still wet. He opened the refrigerator and withdrew a bottle of water.

"What's that for?" Ray gestured to the gym bag slung over Brent's shoulder.

"I thought I'd run to the gym later if Mike doesn't mind me borrowing his truck." Brent took a swig of the water.

"Why don't you drive separately?" Ray suggested, handing one of the travel mugs to Mike.

"Why? I'll only be gone a couple of hours. Is it okay, Mike?"

"Sure." Mike set the mug down and rolled up the blueprints. He rarely let someone else drive his truck, but it would be better if he didn't ride alone with Ray to the site anyway.

"Cool." Brent was the first one out the door.

Mike glanced at Ray. The disappointed expression on Ray's handsome face gave Mike hope. It seemed Ray wanted to be alone with him. "It'll be okay."

Out of Brent's sight, Ray gave Mike another quick kiss. "I'm not sure anymore."

Mike gave Ray's hand a reassuring squeeze before tucking the blueprints under his arm. He wasn't at all surprised to find Brent sitting in the middle of the front seat. Although there was a backseat in his pickup, every time they drove somewhere, Brent always insisted on sitting between Mike and Ray.

"I thought you said we were in a hurry. Let's go." Brent stashed his drink bottle between his legs, once again drawing Mike's attention to his cock. The devilish grin on his face told Mike that Brent knew exactly what he'd done.

The moment Ray got in and shut the door, Mike backed out of the garage. He hit the opener and waited for the door to lower completely before pulling out of the driveway.

"I thought I'd grill some steaks tonight," Ray said as they headed towards the construction site.

"As much as you like to cook, why not open a restaurant instead of an athletic club?" Mike glanced down when he felt Brent's hand on his thigh. *Eight minutes.* He prayed for the strength not to get hard in the eight minutes it would take to get where they were going.

"The gym was my idea. There's nothing sexier than watching sweaty men work out." Brent moved his hand higher. "Besides, it's mostly my money that's paying for it, and Ray knows a good deal when he sees one." He put his free hand on Ray's leg. "Right, honey?"

Ray nodded. "I enjoy cooking, and I'd like to keep it that way. I know if I had to deal with temperamental chefs and wait staff, it wouldn't be the same for me anymore. When Brent came up with the idea for the athletic club, I did some research and agreed it would be profitable if done right. In this area, you can charge a premium for privacy. Making Brookside Athletic Club an invitation-only gym almost assures success."

"Do you already have clients interested?" Mike had never heard of an athletic club that was exclusive to gay men.

"Two hundred and sixty-four at last count and the place isn't even built yet," Brent informed Mike. "When Ray suggested we set a cap of five hundred members, I thought he was crazy, but it's been our biggest draw, in my opinion."

"Huh." Mike felt Brent's hand on his groin. He stopped at a red light and looked down as Brent openly kneaded the front of his jeans. A quick glance at Ray and Mike was shocked to see him glancing out the side window, obviously oblivious of Brent's action. He brushed Brent's hand away, trying not to make a big deal of it.

Brent gave him a dirty look before turning his attentions to Ray. Mike tried to bite his tongue as Brent made a production out of kissing Ray.

The cement truck was already waiting on them when Mike pulled in. He waved at the driver before parking behind the construction trailer they'd rented. He shut off the engine, climbed out and opened the back door. He stared at the kissing men and realised he was more than a little jealous. *Hell.* He grabbed a light jacket out of the backseat along with his hardhat. Mike stepped back to close the door. "I'll see the two of you in a bit."

* * * *

"He pushed my hand away," Brent grumbled, getting out of the truck.

"Serves you right. Mike's told you more than once that he wasn't interested. You're lucky he didn't punch you in the face." After the kiss he'd shared with

Mike earlier, and the stress of the last few days with Brent, Ray wasn't sure what he wanted anymore. He grabbed his hardhat out of the back and slammed the door.

"He's just playing hard to get." Instead of following Ray, Brent headed towards the trailer. "I'll be inside."

"If all you're going to do is sit inside, why'd you bother coming?"

"Because I wanted to see how far I could go on the drive." Brent walked up the four steps and unlocked the office door. "Join me if you get bored."

Ray put his yellow hardhat on and went in search of Mike. He wasn't sure if Mike was okay with what had happened earlier, but there was no time like the present to find out. "Hey," he greeted, standing beside Mike. "Everything okay?"

Mike took his attention away from the crew he'd hired. "Fine. Where's Brent?"

"In the office. Seems he wasn't interested in the building as much as he was riding next to you on the way over."

Mike returned his attention to the work in front of them. "I'd like to touch you right now."

"Same here," Ray agreed, shoving his hands in his pockets.

"Hey, boss, which section you want poured next?" Franco, the site manager, asked, looking up from his clipboard.

"You have that list I gave you yesterday?"

"Yep, right here." Franco held up the clipboard.

"Then follow it." Mike crossed his arms over his chest. "I hope that guy works out. I don't have time to hold his hand every minute of the day, especially when I'm standing here thinking about the taste of your lips."

Ray chuckled. "Do you always flirt with your customers on the job?"

"First time, but I'm enjoying it." Mike didn't even glance at Ray when he said it. "What about you?"

Ray followed Mike as he moved to the next section. "I think it's the sexiest foreplay I've ever been subjected to."

"I'll have to remember that." Mike took a step forward. "No, read the damn list, Franco! This one!"

"Sorry, boss. Won't happen again."

Mike took off his hardhat and rubbed a hand through his hair. "I can see I'm gonna have to watch him like a hawk."

"If you need to go down there, I'm fine here."

Mike studied Ray for a moment. "Don't go anywhere. I'm not done talking yet."

"In that case, I'd better run and get my jacket from the truck before someone notices my cock."

"Oh, I noticed, believe me." Mike winked before taking off towards the crew of men.

Ray jogged to the pickup and grabbed his coat. He felt momentarily guilty about his verbal foreplay with Mike, but brushed it off. They were just words after all, and for now, at least, he didn't feel like stopping.

* * * *

Instead of letting Brent take the truck, Mike dropped him off at the gym. "Just call when you're ready and either I'll swing by or have Ray take my truck."

"Are you sure you don't want to come in for a workout?" Brent asked, sliding off the seat.

"I'm sure. I prefer to get my exercise on the job." Mike waited for Brent to disappear inside before calling Sidney.

"Hello?"

"Hey, first stage of the foundation is poured, thought you'd like to know." Mike pulled into a local drive-thru to order lunch for him and Ray. "Hang on a sec." He gave his order of burgers and fries before returning his attention to the phone call. Why he felt the need to discuss his troubled mind with Sidney he didn't know, and he refused to analyse himself too closely. "Can I ask you something?"

"Sure."

Mike handed the woman at the window a twenty and waited for his change and food. "What was your opinion of Brent when you met him?" He took the two large Cokes and set them in the cup holders before reaching for the sack of food. "Thanks."

"Brent seemed okay. Not really interested in the business aspect of the athletic club, but he was nice enough, why?"

"I don't know." Mike rubbed the back of his neck. "Something about him just rubs me the wrong way. He's been making passes at me."

"Behind Ray's back?" Sidney sounded shocked.

"No, right in front of him. I've been invited to join the two of them for a threesome," Mike explained.

"Are you going to do it?"

"No. I wouldn't feel right sleeping with Brent just to get to Ray. The really strange thing is, I just dropped Brent off at his gym and he didn't try to touch me once on the drive over. It's like he's doing it only in front of Ray for some reason." Mike cleared his throat. He knew he had to tell Sidney all of it. "I kissed Ray this morning, but I knew almost as soon as I did it that I couldn't continue."

"That bad?"

"No," Mike corrected, "that good. One kiss and I've become a jealous bastard where Ray's concerned. I nearly punched Brent in the fucking face for kissing him after I did this morning."

"Then I think the best thing for you to do is get over Ray by finding someone else to occupy your time while you're down there."

"Yeah." Mike thought of going to one of the local gay bars. He'd never really cared for them, but it was a better alternative than falling for another guy he couldn't have. The selfish part of him wished Brent was out of the picture, but he wasn't, and Mike knew he couldn't come between them and still look himself in the mirror each morning. "I'll look into it."

Sidney was quiet for several moments. "You deserve to be happy."

"Maybe so." Mike took a drink of his Coke, buying time. His phone beeped, indicating another incoming call. "Take care of yourself. I'll call if I need anything."

"I'll be here," Sidney answered.

If only that was the case, Mike thought as he ended his conversation with Sidney. "Hello?" he answered the incoming call.

"It's Ray. I was wondering if you'd do me a huge favour while you're out. I just realised I put Brent's insulin kit in my briefcase this morning which should still be in the backseat. Would you mind running it back by the gym for me? It's not always necessary, but I feel better when I know he has it."

Mike pulled into the nearest parking lot. The first time he'd seen Brent inject himself it had given him the willies, he'd never been comfortable around needles. "Sure. I just picked up our lunch, so don't get mad if I eat my fries on the way. Nothing I hate more than cold french fries."

Ray chuckled. "I'd never expect you to eat cold fries."

Mike glanced over his shoulder and spotted Ray's briefcase. "I see it. I'll run it over and be back to the site as soon as I can. If I don't make it there until after lunch, just tell Franco to sit tight."

"Will do, and thanks. I appreciate you making the extra trip."

Mike wanted to tell Ray he was doing it for him, not for Brent, but he figured it would be better to keep his mouth shut. "No problem." He hung up and tossed the phone onto the seat beside him.

Ten minutes later, Mike parked in the gym's parking lot. He retrieved the insulin kit from Ray's briefcase and carried it into the building. Stepping up to the receptionist, Mike held up the small black case. "I need to get this insulin to one of your members, Brent Atwood."

The woman smiled, obviously familiar with the name. "You can go on back. If Brent's not in the workout room, you'll find him in either the sauna or the locker room."

"Thanks." Mike had hoped the woman would take care of delivering the kit, but evidently she trusted Mike to roam around the facility. The lack of security was something he'd mention to Ray in regards to Brookside Athletic Club.

After a quick walk-through of the exercise rooms, Mike headed towards the men's locker room. He didn't immediately see Brent and started to leave when he heard Brent's voice.

"Yeah, fuck yeah, suck that cock," Brent groaned.

Shit. Mike took a deep breath, unsure of what to do. When he heard not one, but two other male voices, Mike started to feel sick to his stomach. Was this a normal occurrence for Brent? Ray told Mike that the gym was Brent's favourite place to be, now Mike had a good idea why. One thing was certain; Ray had no idea what Brent was up to. Anger began to boil up in Mike.

Another series of moans and groans prompted Mike into action. He rounded the corner and stood in front of the opaque glass shower door. Blowing out a calming breath, Mike reached for the handle and jerked the door open.

With one man kneeling in front of him, sucking his cock, and another fucking his ass, Brent looked at Mike and grinned. "Change your mind about working out?"

Mike couldn't believe the smug expression on Brent's face. He dropped the insulin kit at Brent's feet. "Ray wanted to make sure you had that in case something happened." Trying to remember his place in the equation, Mike slammed the door shut without another word. Oh, hell, no, he couldn't just leave without letting Brent know exactly what he thought of him. "Get one of your fuck buddies to take you home, asshole."

The door opened and Brent walked out, dripping water onto the floor. "If you tell Ray about this, you know it'll only hurt him. Besides, I'll deny it. He's known me a hell of a lot longer than he has you. Who do you think he'll believe?"

"Stay away from me," Mike growled. "Don't talk to me, don't look at me, and by God, if you ever touch me, I'll break your fucking arm." Mike couldn't continue to live at Ray and Brent's place, that much was clear. He turned and left the locker room without a backwards glance. Brent was nothing but trash, but he was probably right. Ray would be hurt. That, more than anything, kept Mike from immediately calling Ray.

Mike got behind the wheel of his pickup and slammed the door. He couldn't get the morning kiss with Ray out of his mind. Could he have misjudged the relationship between Ray and Brent so drastically? Maybe they both took lovers on the side. If that was the case, was it possible for Mike to have something with Ray without including Brent?

"Damn." Mike rested his forehead on the steering wheel. Even if that was the case, he knew he couldn't do it. The best thing for him would be to pack his bags and move to an extended stay hotel for the duration of the job. Actually, the wisest decision would be to hightail it back to Chicago, but he'd never walked away from a job before, and he didn't plan to start now.

* * * *

Ray glanced across the front seat at Mike. He wasn't sure what had happened between Mike and Brent, but Mike had been different since returning with Ray's cold lunch. "Did Brent try something?"

Mike took his gaze off the road and glanced at Ray. "With me? No."

Ray stretched his arm out across the back of the seat and put a hand on Mike's shoulder. It wasn't a sexual overture, he simply needed the closeness he'd felt earlier in the day. "What's going on then?"

"I can't be around Brent anymore. I'm not trying to hurt you, but I don't...hell, Ray, I don't like the guy, and, I think it might be better to find somewhere else to stay."

"I know Brent can be pushy, but he'll eventually give up."

Mike shook his head. "At this point, I only have two choices, move out and finish the job or quit and go back to Chicago." He started to reach for Ray's hand but pulled back. "I guess this means we should stop flirting. Kissing is definitely out of the question."

Ray looked away and stared out the passenger window. The realisation that he'd just lost all hope of being with Mike hurt. The pain he felt had him questioning his commitment to Brent. As much as he wished he could say otherwise, his relationship with his partner had to come first. "I guess so. Brent and I agreed a long time ago that we'd only bring another in if it was with the two of us."

Mike made a sound deep in his throat that Ray took as disappointment; at least he hoped it was. Ray released his hold on Mike's shoulder. "I really wish you wouldn't move out. I've enjoyed your company. I'll tell Brent your answer is no, and ask him not to bother you about it again." Ray crossed his fingers it would be enough to get Mike to stay.

Mike stopped at a red light and glanced at Ray. "It's gonna take every ounce of strength I have just to work with you. There's no way I can live with you with this attraction between us." The light turned green and Mike took off once again.

When Mike turned in the direction of the house instead of the gym, Ray spoke up. "Did you forget about picking up Brent?"

"Nope. He's getting a ride home." Mike's jaws clenched and Ray wondered, again, what had happened between Mike and Brent.

"Are you planning to take off as soon as we get back to the house?" Ray couldn't even look at Mike when he asked the question.

"Yeah. I've already made a reservation at the Residence Inn on the Plaza." Mike pulled into Ray's driveway and parked in front of the garage without bothering to pull inside. It felt incredibly final. "You need to know how much I wish things could've worked out between the two of us," Mike began.

Ray opened the door. "You're not the only one."

* * * *

Mike finished unpacking before grabbing a can of beer from the twelve pack he'd bought after leaving Ray's place. Ray's dejected expression as he'd helped Mike load his stuff into the truck still weighed heavily on him. If only Brent wasn't such an asshole.

Stretching out on the couch, Mike's hand hovered over the phone in his pocket. He was tempted to call Ray to make sure Brent had arrived home safely. Mike's concern wasn't for Brent's sake, but because he knew Ray would worry. Giving in to the urge, he grabbed his phone.

"Hey," Ray answered. "Did you forget something?"

"No." Mike didn't want to admit he was calling to check-up on Brent. "Was Brent angry I moved out?"

"Guess so. He called and said he was going to Buddies."

"Buddies?" It was a name Mike hadn't heard. Was it one of the guys he'd seen Brent with in the shower?

"It's a bar he likes to go to when he's pissed at me," Ray explained. "I was sitting here trying to decide whether or not to go after him."

The idea that Brent would be angry with Ray infuriated Mike, especially after what he'd seen earlier in the day. *Sonofabitch.* He may not have enough guts to tell Ray that Brent was fucking around on him, but he had half a mind to let Ray witness Brent's true nature first-hand. Mike slammed his head against the wall behind him. He couldn't do it, no matter how much he hated Brent. "I'll go talk to him if you want me to."

"That's not necessary, but you can come along if you want?"

Mike had a good idea of what Ray would find, and couldn't let him go alone. "Sure," he finally conceded. "I'll go with you."

"I'll call you when I pull up out front. I think I'll take a shower first, so it'll probably be thirty minutes or so."

"I'll be ready." Mike ended the call and groaned. Instead of taking a shower, he decided to call Sidney. God, he needed to break the imaginary bond he had with him.

"Hi," Sidney answered, obviously in a good mood.

"I have a problem."

"With the design?"

Mike smiled. "No, with that other issue I told you about earlier."

"Oh, the threesome thing. What's up?"

"I caught Brent fucking around with two men in the showers at the gym earlier. That pretty much cemented his fate as far as I'm concerned, so I told Ray I couldn't go through with it and moved into a hotel."

"Okay. So what's the problem?"

Mike outlined the situation and waited for Sidney's words of wisdom.

"That's fucked up," Sidney replied.

Despite the serious nature of the situation, Mike couldn't help but grin. "That's all you got?"

"Yeah, I mean, no matter what you do, it sounds like Ray's going to get hurt. So, would it be easier for him to hear it from you or see it first hand?"

"Neither," Mike mumbled. He heard Nash's voice in the background. *What am I doing? Sidney isn't my boyfriend*, he silently admonished himself. "You know what, I'll figure this out. You go back to whatever it was you were doing when I called."

"Sorry, I got home late and we're just sitting down to dinner," Sidney explained.

"No need to apologise. I'll talk to you later." Mike hung up and set the phone on the coffee table.

Getting to his feet, he decided to take a quick shower after all. He undressed quickly and turned on the shower. Mike stood under the warm spray and braced his hands against the tiled wall. With his head down, he groaned as the hot water cascaded over him. *Think.* He had several options, but none left his hands clean. *Dammit!* He wished he didn't know what Brent had done. His only saving grace was the fact that he'd learned Brent's secret only a few hours earlier. At least it was early enough to confess to Ray, and pray Ray forgave him for not telling him immediately.

The guilt that threatened to swallow him came from his own eagerness to get Ray away from Brent. In less than fifteen minutes he'd have the chance, but could he live with himself afterwards?

Chapter Three

When Ray pulled up in front of the hotel lobby, Mike was waiting. For the umpteenth time that day, Ray's body reacted to the handsome older man. *Not going to happen*, he told himself.

Mike opened the door and folded his tall frame into the Nissan 370Z. Ray put the car in gear, but before he could pull onto the street, Mike stopped him with a hand on his arm. "We need to talk."

Ray's hopes soared as his heart started to race. "Have you changed your mind?"

"Is there somewhere quiet we can go and have a drink?"

Ray stared at Mike for several moments. Although Mike hadn't denied he'd changed his mind, his expression left Ray pensive. "What's going on?"

Mike pointed towards an empty parking spot. "Pull in there."

Ray did as asked and turned off the engine. He unfastened his seatbelt and turned to face Mike. "You're starting to worry me."

Mike rubbed his hands together, clearly uncomfortable. He eventually sighed and leaned his head back against the seat. "The last thing in the world I want is to hurt you, but I need you to know that I caught Brent in the shower at the health club earlier today and he wasn't alone."

Ray felt the words like a physical assault. "What do you mean he wasn't alone?"

Mike started to reach for him, but Ray shrank back. "Tell me," Ray demanded.

"He was getting double teamed."

It wasn't until Ray tasted copper that he realised he'd bitten a hole in his bottom lip. Without a word, he leaned over and withdrew a paper napkin from the glove box. He dabbed at the small cut while he tried to come to terms with the news. On several occasions he'd suspected Brent had cheated, but each time he asked, Brent turned the situation around, making Ray feel like the bad guy for accusing him of such a thing. Tossing the napkin to the floor, Ray fired up the sports car. "I need to see it for myself, but I want to do it alone." Frankly, he couldn't stand the thought of Mike seeing his humiliation again.

"Are you sure?" Mike reached for the door handle.

"I'm sure. Sounds like Brent and I have some things to work out. It'll be better if we do that alone." Ray couldn't drive off without asking, "Did he see you?"

"Yeah," Mike mumbled.

"What did he say?" Ray gripped the steering wheel tighter, trying to control his temper.

"First he asked me to join them, then he said you wouldn't believe me if I told you." Mike made no move to open the passenger door. "I'm sorry I had to be the one to tell you, but I couldn't let you walk into that bar blind, knowing what you might find."

Ray soothed the cut on his lip with the tip of his tongue. "I need to see it for myself," he repeated, "but I'm not sure how I'll react once I do."

"Perfectly understandable."

Ray glanced at Mike. He didn't dare confess what the loss of his relationship could mean. Not only was his heart involved, but also every dollar of his savings was tied up either in the house or the athletic club. Still, his money was nothing compared to the investment Brent had put in. Shame assaulted him. How could he think about money when his world had just been rocked by Mike's admission? A thought suddenly occurred to him. "Would you've told me about Brent if I'd stayed home tonight?"

"To be honest, I don't know. I guess I was hoping Brent would go home and make things right." Mike glanced at Ray. "When you told me he'd gone out, I knew he wasn't sorry for what he'd done earlier."

Ray nodded. He understood Mike's position, but it didn't help the churning in his gut. "I'll give you a call once I figure out what the hell is going on."

Mike opened the door, but turned back to Ray before getting out. "I'm sorry. I didn't want this."

Ray clapped Mike on the back. "I know you didn't. This is my mess to figure out." He watched as Mike got out of the car and stood on the sidewalk in front of the hotel. Ray waved before pulling out.

He exited the parking lot and headed to Buddies. There were a number of scenarios running through his mind on the drive. If Brent was going behind his back to cheat, did that mean Ray could see Mike without feeling guilty? Frustrated, Ray knew he couldn't continue his partnership with Brent in that type of environment. He'd already compromised his beliefs on monogamy by bringing other men into their bed in an effort to keep Brent happy. There was no way he could live with himself if he allowed Brent to stray outside of their relationship.

Ray parked the car and got out before he could talk himself out of facing the truth. Stepping inside, it didn't take him long to spot Brent. Bare chested, he was leaning against one of the pool tables, another man's tongue down his throat. Bile rose in Ray's throat as he watched the stranger openly grind himself against Brent.

As Ray continued to watch the scene, he realised that although he was hurt by Brent's betrayal, he wasn't jealous. Had he become so used to seeing Brent with other men that he no longer cared? He remembered the way he'd felt when Brent had sat on Mike's lap and kissed him that first evening. Although he hadn't been able to put his feelings into words, Ray now understood that he had been jealous, but not for the reasons he should have been.

Ray quickly settled into the realisation that he wanted Mike more than he'd probably ever wanted Brent. Knowing Brent had lied to him after everything they'd shared fuelled Ray's resolve. He needed to break away from their unhealthy relationship. He turned and left the bar without making his presence known, leaving Brent to do whatever he wanted.

Ray drove home in a daze. There were things he needed to take care of before confronting Brent.

* * * *

Ray parked beside the construction trailer. For four days he'd played the part of the dutiful partner, never once letting on that he knew anything of Brent's extracurricular activities. Hardhat in place, Ray walked over to the building site, impressed with the amount of work Mike's crew had accomplished. He just hoped Mike's hard work wouldn't be in vain. "Hey," he said, announcing his presence.

Bent over a set of blueprints, Mike lifted his head and met Ray's gaze. "I've been calling."

Ray nodded in acknowledgement. "I know, but I needed a few days to clear my head." He gestured to the trailer. "Can I talk to you?"

"Definitely." Mike lifted his arm and waved Franco over. "I'll be in the office. Give me a call if you need me."

"Sure thing," Franco replied before going back to work.

"How's he doing?" Ray asked as they started towards the office.

"Better." Mike stuffed his hands in his jacket pockets. "So what's going on?"

Ray opened the trailer door and preceded Mike into the office. "I've been talking to the bank."

"Something wrong?"

"You could say that. We put the house up as collateral for the building loan. Problem is, the house is in Brent's name, so if he pulls out, I'm screwed. Fortunately, I own the land free and clear, so he can't continue the build without me, but I'm having a hard time convincing the bank to give me the loan."

"What's Brent say?" Mike crossed his arms and leaned against the desk.

"He doesn't know anything about it. I had to do some fast talking to convince the bank not to call him." Days spent with little sleep had Ray on edge, but he kept telling himself it was the right thing to do.

"What does that mean, are you breaking up?"

Although Ray had run through it a hundred times in his head over the last several days, he'd yet to admit it out loud. "I can't trust him with my love anymore, and if I can't trust him with that, how am I supposed to trust him with anything?"

Mike pushed away from the desk and moved to stand in front of Ray. "I'm sorry."

Ray wanted nothing more than to wrap his arms around Mike, but he couldn't do it, not yet anyway. "I know I should've talked to Brent by now, but I have a feeling things'll get nasty, and I'm not financially ready for that yet."

"Be honest with me, what does this mean for the future of the project?" Mike asked.

"I don't have the kind of collateral it takes to fund something of this size on my own. I've called a few people that I think might be interested, but so far I haven't heard back from anyone." Ray held his breath. Mike had every right to shut down the build until Ray could prove he had the money to pay Shriver Construction for what he owed.

"What about Brent, you think he'll fight ya for this?"

Ray shook his head. "Maybe, but not because he wants it. If he fights me, it'll be because he has the money to do it."

Mike rested his hands on his hips. "I can float you for a couple of weeks, but you gotta tell Brent."

"I appreciate it, and you're right, I won't know what kind of shit I'll be in until I talk to him."

"And I can't kiss you again until you do," Mike added.

Ray smiled for the first time in days. "I'm looking forward to that." He wasn't delusional, he knew Mike's life was in Chicago, but that didn't keep him from wanting more than he probably should.

"It's almost quittin' time, can I interest you in dinner?"

The churning in Ray's stomach that had been a constant presence in recent days, began to settle at the request. "Yeah, I'd like that."

* * * *

Mike dipped the warm tortilla chip into the spicy sauce, without taking his eyes off Ray. There were questions he wanted to ask, but Ray looked so at peace he hated to ruin it. One thing had become perfectly clear to Mike in the days since Ray had become aware of Brent's infidelity; he wanted Ray in his life. So much, in fact, that he hadn't longed for Sidney once since watching Ray drive out of the parking lot that night.

"I'll have to find a new place to live," Ray announced.

An offer to stay with him was on the tip of Mike's tongue but he swallowed the words before they escaped. Although he would love to spend every moment he was in town with Ray, Mike knew it was important for Ray to get his confidence back. Brent had really done a number on the poor guy over the years, and Ray would need time to heal. "What did you have in mind?"

Ray shrugged. "The cheapest apartment I can find for now."

The answer brought up one of the questions Mike was dying to ask. "Why's the athletic club so important to you? I'm sure you could sell the land and get your savings back and then some."

Ray didn't answer right away. He dunked another chip and ate it, obviously trying to put his thoughts into words. "Several reasons, really. I've worked for nearly three years trying to get the idea to the stage it is now. I don't mean to sound conceited, but I'm the one who's done all the leg work, and I'd rather not hand it over to Brent without a fight." Ray picked up his Coke and took a drink. "I also need to feel like I've accomplished something in the last seven years. Losing my teaching position was tough, but it was completely my fault, so I tried to accept it and move on. I'm not getting any younger, and I guess I need something to show for my life."

Although he'd promised himself he wouldn't make their shared dinner an actual date, Mike couldn't resist reaching across the table to cover Ray's hand with his. He completely understood Ray's reasoning, he'd felt much the same way lately regarding Sidney. It was a shitty thing to realise you'd wasted a good part of your life on something that would never happen. "I'll do what I can to help."

Ray turned his hand over and threaded his fingers through Mike's. "Thanks. Can we talk about something else now? Reality will rear its ugly head any moment and pull me back down into the troubled pit I've found myself in lately, but at least for now, I want to enjoy your company."

"Absolutely," Mike agreed.

They spent the next hour talking about Kansas City and everything it had to offer. Mike was ashamed to admit he really knew nothing about the area. Six months earlier if someone had mentioned Kansas, Dorothy and Toto would've immediately come to mind, but after spending a short time in the city, he was beginning to like it more all the time.

Brent called twice during dinner, but both times Ray sent it straight to voicemail. When it rang for the third time, Ray picked up the phone and closed his eyes after glancing at the display. "Sorry, but I should probably take this."

"Go ahead. I'll take care of the bill." Mike gestured for the waiter as he tried his best not to eavesdrop.

"No, I'm not cooking, which is why I left you the message earlier about finding something to eat on your own," Ray said into the phone. "Then go to the store or a drive-thru." He rolled his eyes. "Fine, I'll pick you up something on the way home. We need to talk anyway."

Mike handed the waiter his credit card after looking over the bill.

Ray set the phone onto the table with a weary sigh. "I guess tonight's the night, because I can't pretend anymore."

"In that case, go out with me on Friday." It was only two days away, but Mike hoped Ray would be in a place emotionally where he could enjoy himself for an evening.

"Can I call you tomorrow about it?" Ray asked. "I honestly have no idea what I'm about to walk into, and breaking a date isn't the way I want to start things with you."

Mike signed the charge slip before standing. "Come on, I'll walk you to your car."

On the way to the parking lot, Mike couldn't resist holding Ray's hand. "I can't wait until I can kiss you again."

Ray unlocked his car. "Mentally, I left Brent days ago. I can't see that one kiss would hurt."

Mike took a quick glance around the lot before pulling Ray into his arms. He wasted no time sealing their lips together and within seconds, his tongue was exploring the interior of Ray's mouth. The kiss did more than ratchet up his physical need for Ray, it cemented his emotional connection to the man.

When the need to rub himself against Ray became too great, Mike broke the kiss and stepped back. "I could do that all night."

"Me, too," Ray agreed. "Thanks for dinner." He opened his car door and got in, but before he could shut it, Mike bent down for one more kiss.

Mike slid his tongue across Ray's, relishing every moment. "Give me a call after you talk to Brent and let me know you're okay."

Ray licked his bottom lip. "I will."

* * * *

Ray left his briefcase in the car and carried the sack of fast food into the house. He set the bag on the kitchen island and took off his coat. "Dinner's here," he announced.

"I'm watching *American Idol*, bring it in," Brent returned.

Ray ground his teeth and grabbed Brent's dinner. He walked into the family room and dropped the sack on the coffee table.

"What, nothing to drink?"

Ray glanced at the empty beer cans. "Doesn't look like you need anything else." Instead of sitting on the couch beside Brent, Ray chose the recliner. "We need to talk."

"Can it wait 'til commercial?"

"No." Ray reached for the remote before Brent could and turned off the television.

"I was wondering when he'd tell you," Brent said between bites of his cheeseburger.

"That's all you have to say?"

Brent licked his fingers. "It didn't mean anything, just sex. It has nothing to do with our relationship."

Ray couldn't believe Brent didn't even have enough guilt to apologise. "It had everything to do with our relationship. I compromised my entire belief system to make you happy. Do you honestly think I ever wanted another man in our bed?"

Brent grinned. "Where were you tonight? With Mike, right?" He chuckled. "I think you just contradicted yourself."

"I haven't slept with Mike. Not because I didn't want to, but because he can't stand you, and I told him I couldn't do anything without you. Then I find out you're fucking strangers at the gym."

"They weren't strangers," Brent corrected.

"That's even worse." Ray leant forward in his chair. "What about the two men who were all over you at Buddies the other night? Were they the same ones from the shower?"

"No, and I don't know who you have spying on me, but all we did was kiss."

"I don't need a spy. I saw you with my own eyes."

Brent shrugged, apparently unconcerned. "You're making a mountain out of a mole hill. And what the fuck do you mean Mike can't stand me? He sure seemed okay when he had his tongue down my throat that first night."

"That was before he got to know you."

"So, what, just because he doesn't like me all the sudden you're having issues with me? Open your eyes, Ray, he's trying to break us up so he can have you for himself," Brent argued.

"Mike didn't fuck another man, you did. If he's guilty of anything it's opening my eyes."

"To what? I'm here tonight, isn't that what you like, to stay home and be boring together? Do you honestly think that's an easy thing for me to do?" Brent moved to kneel beside Ray's chair. "Don't do what I think you're about to do. Sure we have our problems, but don't let this guy come in and fill your head with a bunch of bullshit."

Staring down at Brent, Ray realised what had gone wrong with their relationship. "You know, I think we've tried so hard to change for each other that neither of us are happy. I love you, but I don't think I've loved myself since the first night you brought someone else over to share our bed. I'm not that kind of person, but I tried to be for you."

"You're not the only one. I've sacrificed, too."

"I know. That's what I'm saying. You've tried to become the kind of partner I need by staying home for quiet nights in and stuff, but it's obviously not working for you or else you wouldn't be asking me for threesomes and fucking guys at the gym." Instead of being angry or upset, Ray felt resigned. It was a realisation that he and Brent should've parted ways years earlier.

"So what now, are you really breaking up with me?" Brent rested his cheek on Ray's knee.

"Yeah, I am, but it doesn't have to be a bad thing. We can still go on as business partners if you think we can get along enough to make it work." The discussion wasn't what Ray had expected, and he started to wonder if the days of worrying had been pointless.

"I'm supposed to look at you and talk to you every day knowing you're fucking someone else?"

Ray tried to remain calm at the question. "Evidently you've been fucking someone else for quite a while. If

I can make a business partnership work between us, why can't you?"

Brent got to his feet and walked over to the bar in the corner of the room to pour himself a glass of whisky. "The difference is I've never been emotionally involved with anyone but you, and for some reason I can't get you to understand that." He downed the drink in one shot before pouring another. "It hurts to think of you loving someone else."

Ray joined Brent at the bar and poured himself a glass of red wine. "You need things that I can't give you, and I need someone who wants me and only me. If there's a way for us to remain friends, I want that, but if you don't think that's possible, I'll respect that, too." He stopped himself before telling Brent he'd do whatever it took to hang onto the athletic club. If the two of them could work it out between them, it would be easier. A legal battle could not only drag on but it could get very expensive.

"What about the house?"

"It's your house," Ray acknowledged. "I'll find an apartment that I can afford."

"You could just stay here if you want. We've got plenty of bedrooms."

Ray loved the house, but not enough to put himself in the position to witness Brent's single lifestyle. "I think it would be better for me to move out. Working together might prove hard enough, living together could be disastrous if you really want to remain friends."

Brent set down his drink and wrapped his arms around Ray. "I love you. I'm begging you not to do this."

Ray reciprocated the affectionate gesture. "Do you honestly think you can be happy in a strictly monogamous relationship? Because that's what I need."

"I know you think Mike'll give you that, and maybe he can for a while, but there's no way he'll give up his family business to move here. Even if he did, he won't stay faithful, I'm sorry, Ray, but you're not that good."

Although Ray had questioned his own talents in the bedroom, it was the first time Brent had ever mentioned it. The criticism stung. He swallowed the hurt, putting the pain away for another day. "Maybe you're right, but I have to reach for what I want or it'll never be within my grasp."

* * * *

Mike pulled into the jobsite and was surprised to see Ray's car parked beside the office. He'd slept with his cell phone next to his bed in case Ray needed someone to talk to, but had slept through the night without the desired call.

Franco's rust-eaten truck came to a squealing stop next to Mike. "Hey, boss."

Mike nodded, his mind still on Ray. "Morning." He gestured to the office. "I'll be inside, give me a call if you need something."

"Will do." Franco grabbed his tool belt and hardhat and headed towards the building site. Despite Mike's earlier reservations about Franco's abilities, he'd proved to be a real asset to the project and framing was moving along nicely.

Mike entered the trailer and found Ray asleep on the small couch, using the small throw Brent had left for a blanket and his coat for a pillow. For the first time, Mike got a good look of Ray's muscular body. Clad only in a pair of black boxer briefs, Ray's body looked amazing. Although he never mentioned working out, it was obvious Ray did something to take such good care of himself.

Deciding to let the tired man sleep, Mike set about making a pot of coffee. As quietly as he could, Mike used a jug of bottled water to fill the automatic coffeemaker.

"Hey."

Mike glanced over his shoulder to find Ray sitting up on the couch, his chest still bare and his hair in disarray. "You should've called." He spooned grounds into the filter and flipped the switch before turning to face Ray.

Ray scratched his head before popping his neck. "I wouldn't have been good company."

"So, I take it you talked to Brent." Instead of sitting beside Ray, Mike moved his desk chair over.

"Yeah."

"How'd that go?"

"As well as can be expected, I guess. He seemed more hurt than anything." Ray rested his elbows on his knees and bent to scrub his face with his hands. "I'm not gonna lie, it was hard. A couple of times, I almost changed my mind about leaving."

"So, why didn't you?" Mike knew he didn't have the right to ask, but he needed to know where Ray's head was at.

"Because in all his pleas, he never once promised to be faithful." Ray looked up at Mike. "And then there's you."

"What about me?"

Ray stood and crossed to stand in front of Mike. He gestured to Mike's lap. "You mind?"

Mike uncrossed his arms and held them out, welcoming Ray's company. "Not at all."

Ray straddled Mike's legs and sat facing him. "I can't stop thinking about you." He brushed Mike's hair off his forehead before kissing Mike's suntanned skin. "Even though it makes me feel guilty as hell, I want you."

Mike pulled Ray closer to his chest. "Nothing to feel guilty about. You did the right thing by ending one relationship before starting another."

Ray kissed Mike's cheeks before moving to his lips. "Is that what we're doing, starting a relationship?" he whispered against Mike's lips.

Mike rubbed his palms against Ray's bare back. He wanted more from Ray than was logistically possible, but he wasn't about to rule anything out. "I hope so."

With a hand against the back of Ray's head, Mike closed the distance between them. He swept the interior of Ray's mouth with his tongue as Ray began to unbutton his shirt. Mike's cock hardened at the thought of making love to Ray after the many nights he'd spent dreaming about it.

Ray began to kiss his way down Mike's neck, eventually sliding off his lap to kneel between his legs. Instead of zeroing in on the erection pressing against Mike's fly, Ray concentrated on Mike's chest. He ran his fingers through Mike's salt-and-pepper-coloured chest hair, taking the time to pinch each nipple as he explored. "I like this," he said, rubbing his cheek against the coarse hair.

Mike brushed the back of his hand across Ray's torso. He was surprised by how smooth Ray's chest was for a man of Italian heritage.

"It's waxed. Brent insisted on it," Ray replied, obviously reading Mike's thoughts.

Mike circled one of Brent's nipples with his fingertip, enjoying the way the tiny nub hardened and puffed under his touch. "Don't do it anymore, unless you like it."

With a grin on his face, Ray began to knead Mike's cock through his jeans. "You like hairy men?"

Mike unfastened the top snap on his jeans. "I like a man to be comfortable with who he is, especially when that man is you."

Ray took over and unzipped Mike's jeans. "That'll take some getting used to."

Mike spied Ray's suitcase beside the couch. "Please tell me you have lube and condoms with you?"

Nodding, Ray fished Mike's cock out of the confines of his jeans. Starting at the base, Ray licked a path up the length to capture the head between his lips.

"Mmm," Mike groaned. It had been a long time since he'd had someone pleasure him. He stared down at Ray, seeing more than a sexual partner. The way Ray's lips stretched over Mike's thick cock was a huge turn-on, and Mike couldn't resist reaching down to soothe the corner of Ray's mouth with his finger. "Feels good."

Ray looked up and met Mike's gaze, burying Mike's cock as far down his throat as it would go. Ray's gag reflex kicked in, constricting the muscles surrounding Mike's length. Pulling back, Ray released Mike's cock and shook his head. "You're a lot bigger than Brent."

Oddly, Mike felt a sense of pride rush through him at the declaration. He'd worried how he could compete with Brent in the bedroom, the man was just so young and gorgeous, but it seemed Mike held a secret weapon that Ray appeared to be impressed with. The thought of stretching Ray's ass as he pumped his cock in and out fuelled Mike's lust. "Stand up, I've got an idea."

Still holding Mike's cock in his hand, Ray got to his feet. "What did you have in mind?"

Mike reached out, grabbed the elastic waistband of Ray's underwear, and pulled them down, freeing a nice-sized erection. "I've never fucked someone on a jobsite, but I don't think I can wait any longer."

"You want me to lock the door?"

"Shit. I can't believe I didn't think of that earlier." Mike couldn't imagine what would've happened had Franco or one of the other contractors walked in.

With a chuckle, Ray walked over and locked the door before closing the blind beside Mike's desk. "That should do it."

"Not quite." Mike shrugged out of his shirt and tossed it onto the desk. He started to toe off his boots, but Ray stopped him.

"Leave them on. If you had any idea how many times I've driven by construction sites and lusted after the faceless men in hardhats." Ray gave a dramatic body shiver. "Yeah, leave them on."

Mike grinned. "You want me to go get my tool belt, too?"

"No, but if you had it on you, I'd ask you to leave it." Ray bit his bottom lip. "Is that too weird?"

Mike would definitely have to play construction worker with Ray in the very near future. "I'll take it home with me tonight."

"Deal." Ray stripped out of his underwear and stood in front of Mike looking incredibly comfortable in his nudity. He gestured towards Mike. "Feel free to join me. You can take those off, too." He gestured to Mike's boots. "I'll wait for the tool belt."

"If you're sure." Mike stopped drooling over Ray long enough to take off his boots, jeans and underwear. While Ray dug into his suitcase for supplies, Mike moved to the couch. He couldn't get over the perfection of Ray's body. "Are you sure you're forty?"

Ray stood and held up a box of condoms and a bottle of lube. "Forty-two, actually, but I come from a long line of angry Italians who live longer than they probably should."

Mike could tell there was a story there that he'd need to ask about when the time was right, but at the moment, his cock seemed to be doing all the thinking. He moved to the edge of the sofa and gestured for Ray to lay down. Not knowing how long it had been since Ray had bottomed, Mike wanted to take his time getting Ray stretched enough to take his cock without pain.

With his cock still hard from Ray's earlier blowjob and the thought of what was to come, Mike rolled the condom down his length. He set the bottle of lube beside his knee and manoeuvred himself between Ray's spread thighs.

Ray moved to rest one leg on the back of the sofa. "I need you to know I didn't come here for this."

The statement gave Mike pause. "I didn't think you did. I'd like to believe you came because you knew I'd welcome you." He swiped the tip of Ray's cock with his tongue while lubing his fingers. Ray's body jerked when Mike touched his puckered hole. "How long's it been?"

"A while. I always forget how much I enjoy it until it happens."

Mike rimmed Ray's hole several times before slowly pushing the tip of his finger inside. As Ray's eyelids fluttered at the invasion, Mike realised Ray was a natural bottom, trying to satisfy Brent for years by topping. He eased his finger deeper, watching Ray carefully.

Ray moaned and began to caress his own chest. "I knew those calloused hands would feel good," he mumbled.

Mike poured more lube onto his fingers before adding another. "You look so sexy riding my fingers," he said when Ray started to move. He continued the slow process of stretching Ray until he was satisfied the muscles were properly loosened.

After rubbing the excess lube onto his sheathed cock, Mike positioned the crown at Ray's hole. "Ready."

"More than I think I've ever been." Ray continued to rub a path back and forth between his nipples, taking time to give each nub a pinch before moving back. With his free hand, Ray stroked his erection as Mike slowly pushed through the ring of muscles.

"God, you're tight." Mike ground his teeth as he tried to control the desire to push in to the hilt. He rocked his hips back and forth until his cock was buried to the root inside Ray. "Ahhh, fuck."

Ray took several calming breaths before tapping Mike's hip with his hand. "Ready."

Mike lifted Ray's legs and draped them over his shoulders. He started slow, moving his length in and out of Ray's body, in an attempt to make the moment last. With each thrust, Mike prayed he'd finally found a man who could completely fill his heart.

"Harder," Ray begged.

Mike withdrew his cock and pulled Ray onto the floor. He positioned them so that Ray's upper body rested on the sofa cushions and Mike could kneel behind the man's ass. "Need more lube?" he asked in Ray's ear, taking the time to suck the tender lobe into his mouth.

"I'm good." Ray stuck out his ass and waited for Mike's cock.

"Yes, you are." Mike lined up and drove inside in one smooth push. *Fuck. I could definitely get used to this.*

With his hands on Ray's hips, Mike began a fast rhythm, his balls slapping against Ray's ass with each thrust. The jarring to one of his most sensitive body parts fuelled Mike's lust like never before. He began to grunt as his hips pistoned back and forth. A tingling began in his balls that had nothing to do with the abuse they were currently suffering. "I'm coming," he said, a second before he lost his tempo.

Ray grabbed for the crumpled shirt shoved into the corner of the couch and covered himself as he cried out with his own release. "Fuck!" he growled.

Mike slumped against Ray's back as his cock continued to shoot cum into the condom. Between the two of them, the panting inside the small office was almost deafening. Rubbing his cheek against Ray's sweaty back, Mike realised it was the first time in years he'd fucked a man without imagining at least once that the man under him was Sidney. He wrapped his hand around the base of the condom and withdrew from Ray's heated body before rolling onto his back.

Once Mike recovered, he stood and snatched a tissue out of the box on the desk. He wrapped the condom up and threw it away before reaching for his jeans. He hated to leave Ray after one of the best fucks of his life, but he expected Franco to call or pound on the door at any minute. "Do I still have to wait until tomorrow to take you out?"

Seated on the floor with his back against the couch, Ray chuckled. "No, but I've got to get out of here and find somewhere to live."

"You can stay with me if you need to." Mike zipped his jeans before picking up his discarded shirt.

"I appreciate it, but I think I'd do better right now in a more stable environment."

Mike tried to hide the pinch of pain the statement elicited. "Yeah, I guess you're right. Unless you think you'll get back together with Brent, that is."

Ray scooted over to his suitcase and began pulling out clean clothes. "I don't think there's a chance of that. But at least for now, we're hoping to remain friends and business partners."

Jealousy began to rear its ugly head. "Given your past with him, do you think that's a good idea?"

"I don't know if it'll work, but at this point I don't have a lot of choice. I've got a lot to lose if this club doesn't get built."

Mike waited to approach Ray until he was almost fully dressed. He wrapped his arms around Ray's waist and pulled him in for a deep kiss, loving the taste of Ray more with each passing second. "I'll do my best to get the project finished ahead of schedule."

Ray smoothed Mike's hair into place. "I'd appreciate that. I'll call you later."

Mike hated to let Ray go, but work called. "Come back by if you get done early."

"I will. If you don't mind, I'd like to use this office until I can get moved into an apartment."

Mike nearly forgot Ray had his own consulting company. "I'd love it, it'll give me a chance to see you more often."

"Perfect. Thanks." Ray gave Mike another heated kiss before pulling away. "Later."

"Later," Mike returned before Ray left the office. He rubbed his hand over his mouth, trying like hell to wipe the goofy-assed grin from his face before joining

Franco on the site. "Get a hold of yourself, you old fool."

He left the trailer feeling better than he had in years.

Chapter Four

Uncomfortable, Ray stood in the foyer as the moving company carried out the furniture Brent had agreed he could take. "Not that table," he told one of the men.

"It's okay," Brent said, stepping into the foyer to join Ray. "It's more your taste than mine anyway."

Although things with Mike were going even better than Ray had expected, he couldn't help but feel guilty every time he was around Brent. "But you bought that one when we were in Aspen three years ago."

"Yeah, but the reason I got it was because you fell in love with it." Brent motioned for the mover to take it out. "Still seeing Mike?"

Ray nodded.

"Does he make you happy?"

"Let's not do this," Ray suggested. "I'm sorry that I've hurt you, but I was hurt, too."

"I know." Brent stood beside Ray with his arms crossed over his chest. "You might as well take those pans you like so much. It's not like I'm planning to cook anytime soon."

Ray had planned a shopping trip to stock up on all the everyday items he'd need, so the offer was a welcome one. "Thanks, I'd appreciate that." He took off towards the kitchen with Brent right behind him. He had to admit he was curious about Brent's sex life since he'd left, but he didn't know that he could handle the answer. He opened the cabinets and began to pull out the professional cookware Brent had purchased when they bought the house. "Would you box these up, too?" he asked one of the guys.

"Sure thing."

"Mom and Dad are coming into town later this week. Mom wants to help me pick out some new furniture." Brent hopped up on the island.

The scene was so commonplace it made Ray even more uncomfortable. He tried to busy himself with gathering the lids for the pots, but it didn't help. "Wait. Why's your dad coming?" Knowing how much Brent's father hated to travel, it didn't bode well for Ray.

"He wants to check on the club," Brent mumbled, his legs swinging back and forth.

"Why would he be interested in the club?" Tightness began to spread its way across Ray's chest.

Brent jumped down and left the room. "Gotta go."

Brent's exit spurned Ray into action. "Oh no you don't." He caught up with Brent before he could open his car door. "What's going on?"

"Dad wants to see for himself if the project's worth sinking more money into or if I'd be better to just take the loss and move on."

"What! You can't do that. We had a deal." Despite all the feelers Ray had put out about looking for another investor, he'd come up empty. If Brent pulled out, there'd be no way Ray could finish the athletic club on his own.

"I'm sorry," Brent whined, "but I don't know anything about running a business, so I asked him what he thought."

"Who said you were going to run it? I thought we'd agreed I'd handle that part of the business." Hands jammed deep into his pockets, Ray began to pace back and forth in front of the garage.

Brent shook his head. "I've been thinking about it, and I know we agreed that I would handle the staff and stuff, but I know I won't be able to be around you all day every day." He stepped in front of Ray. "I still love you, and I want you to come home."

"I can't. I know it's hard right now, but it'll get better. Why don't you let me handle the rest of the construction? Maybe the time apart will do us both some good. In another few months, you'll have moved on to someone else and the two of us can continue to build the dream we've talked about for so long." Ray wasn't used to pleading, but with three years of his time and his life savings wrapped up in the club, there was no way he could walk away from it.

"Is there anything else, Mr DeMonico?"

"You get the pots?" Ray asked without turning to look at the man.

"Yes, sir."

"I guess that's all then." He glanced over his shoulder. "I'll meet you at the apartment." Ray refused to go anywhere until he convinced Brent not to give up their planned venture. "Do me a favour and try to talk your dad out of coming with your mom. Hell, tell him you've changed your mind about everything and you want this to work."

"I can't. You know how my father is. Once he gets something into his head, there's no stopping him. I'm sorry, Ray, I really am, but he'll be onsite first thing Saturday morning, if I know him."

With a feeling of defeat, Ray nodded. "I'll tell Mike." He walked to his car and got in. Ray knew it didn't matter what Brock Atwood really thought of the project, he'd shut it down first chance he got just to spite Ray.

* * * *

A knock at the door interrupted Ray's unpacking, but he didn't mind a bit since he was expecting Mike. He opened the door and smiled. He seemed to do that a lot lately. "Welcome to my new home."

Mike walked in and shut the door behind him. "Bigger than I'd thought it'd be."

"I had to sign a year's lease, so I figured I might as well get something big enough to hold my office." The two bedroom, two bathroom, eighth-floor apartment was two streets off the Country Club Plaza and only eight blocks from Mike's hotel. Ray waved Mike into the kitchen. "I was just finishing up."

Mike whistled when he entered the gourmet kitchen. "This doesn't look very temporary to me."

Ray turned and stared at Mike. Secretly, he'd hoped to make a home of the apartment, tempting Mike to put down roots in Kansas City, but it sounded like Mike didn't approve of his choice. "You don't like it?"

"No, I didn't say that. I just thought you were going to get some little place to hang your hat until you figured out what your next step is, but by the looks of this place, I guess you've already decided."

No longer excited by his new apartment, Ray set the mixing bowl in the cabinet. "Ready to go eat?"

"Sure, if that's what you want." Mike grabbed Ray's hand and pulled him into his arms. "What sounds good?"

Ray had planned to suggest delivered pizza in bed, but with everything that had happened earlier in the day and Mike's reaction to his apartment, he was no longer in the mood. "Doesn't matter. We can take a walk and see what strikes our fancy?"

"I've got a better idea. Why don't we have a picnic at the construction site? You run by and pick up a bucket of chicken or something, and I'll go on to the site and clear us a spot." Mike didn't release Ray immediately. Instead, he lowered his lips to Ray's.

Ray pressed himself against the slightly taller man as he opened for Mike's tongue. One kiss and Ray was putty in Mike's hand. What was it about Mike that made Ray so taken care of with only a sensuous swipe of the tongue?

Mike nipped Ray's bottom lip before breaking the kiss. "Is that a yes?"

The thought of rolling around on a blanket with Mike at the site turned Ray on. "Yeah, I'd like that. Just give me a minute to change my clothes." Ray started to pull away, but Mike held him tighter. "How about I help you get undressed?"

Ray smiled. "I'll show you mine if you show me yours."

* * * *

Mike cleaned the sharp objects out of his tool belt and set them to the side. Because the belt usually rode low on his hips, and Mike had other plans for that particular area of his anatomy, he adjusted it higher on his waist. He'd turned on several of the work lights in the hope that any passerby would think he was burning the midnight oil instead of playing dress up games with his boyfriend. Luckily, the crew had managed to get the last exterior wall in place earlier in the day. He'd even parked his truck, with the Shriver's Construction sign plastered to the side, by the road, praying a nosey cop wouldn't stop to check on the site.

A car door slammed outside, and Mike's nerves kicked in. *What the hell am I doing?* At the last minute, he tossed a cloth tarp over a sawhorse and put the hardhat on his head. He'd had the scene planned for a while, but had waited for the right time. "Tonight's the night," he whispered. "Here's hoping I'm not about to make a fool of myself."

"Mike?" Ray called, entering the building.

"Back here." Mike reached down and unzipped his oldest, rattiest jeans enough to show his pubic hair. He turned around and pretended to measure one of the two by four studs.

"What're you doing?" Ray stepped into the room.

"Figured I might as well get some work done." Mike set the tape measure down and turned to face Ray. "That is what you pay me for, isn't it, boss?"

Ray almost dropped the bucket of chicken and sack of beer, saving them at the last moment and gently setting them to the floor. He stood and continued towards Mike, clearly willing to play out his fantasy scenario. "That's not all I pay you for."

The hungry expression on Ray's face put Mike's fear of looking stupid out of his mind. Mike held his breath in anticipation when Ray stood directly in front of him. Ray reached down and lowered Mike's zipper the rest of the way before tucking the loosened denim under, exposing more of Mike's groin. "Get rid of the shirt," Ray ordered.

Instead of pulling the white undershirt off over his head, Mike grabbed the material at the neck and ripped it down the middle. "Is that all, boss?"

Ray took a step back and stared Mike up and down. "Damn, you're sexy."

Feeling bolder now that he knew Ray wasn't going to laugh at him, Mike rubbed one hand across his chest while sliding the other down the front of his body to pull his cock and balls out of the confines of his jeans. "Every time you visit the site, I dream of bending you over and fucking you as hard as I can. I know a couple of the other guys are thinking the same thing, but I've made it clear that you belong to me."

Ray's eyebrows lifted in surprise. "So you want to put your mark on me, is that it?"

"Oh, I wanna do all kinds of things to you, marking you is only a small part of what I have planned." Mike waited for Ray's response, hoping he hadn't gone too far in the charade.

To Mike's delight, Ray unzipped his jeans. "Did you sweep this floor nice and clean like I told you to?"

"Yes, boss," Mike answered, his cock hardening as Ray began to undress.

Completely naked, Ray reached out and encircled Mike's cock in his hand. "Can you fuck in those clothes?"

Mike nodded, his need for Ray building by the second. It hadn't escaped his attention that they had yet to touch, other than a quick brush of Ray's hand, as he unzipped Mike's jeans. "You gonna kiss me first, or am I just a hired piece of meat to you?"

Ray tilted his head back and swiped his tongue across Mike's closed mouth. "You're so much more than that to me. Game or not, I need you to know that," Ray said, breaking character.

Mike did know, but it was still reassuring to hear. "Then kiss me like you mean it."

Pressing himself against Mike's body, Ray pulled Mike's head down for a kiss. Mike opened immediately to Ray's tongue, groaning at Ray's enthusiasm as the kiss took on a life of its own. Mike grabbed Ray's bare ass and began to grind against him. There was something so sinfully erotic about the way Ray kissed that Mike was putty in his hands in no time.

Mike separated the cheeks of Ray's ass and circled the puckered hole with a dry finger. He broke the kiss and fished two condoms and small bottle of lube from his pocket. "I'm gonna fuck you so hard you won't be able to step foot inside this building without remembering my cock buried in your ass."

Although Mike said the words in character, he meant them. He still wasn't sure where things were headed between the two of them, but he wanted to make a lasting impression on Ray in case it didn't work out.

Ray licked his lips. "Are you really going to need both of those rubbers?"

Mike stepped to the side and motioned towards the covered sawhorse. "Trust me." He pointed towards the drop cloth once more. "Bend over."

Ray tested the sawhorse's sturdiness before bracing both hands on the covered wood. He planted his spread legs on the cement floor and glanced over his shoulder. "Fuck me."

Mike moved to stand behind Ray, coating his fingers with lube at the same time. "I plan to play for a few minutes before I shove my cock up your ass." He circled Ray's asshole with his finger several times, waiting for Ray to relax before slowly pushing inside. "Your body wants me."

"My body...my heart," Ray mumbled, resting his forehead against his arm.

Mike leaned over Ray's back and whispered in his ear. "I'm through playing the game. I want to fuck you as your lover, not your employee."

Ray opened his eyes. "I've never thought of you as an employee. Sorry if I made you think that."

It was obvious Ray took Mike's statement to heart. "You didn't." He kissed Ray's cheek as he added a second finger to his ass. With his free hand, he took off the hardhat and tossed it to the floor.

Ray began to move his hips, pushing back against Mike's hand. "Please."

Mike had planned to draw Ray's pleasure out, but he couldn't ignore the soft plea from Ray's parted lips. He ripped the foil packet open with his teeth and managed to get the condom out and roll it down his length without removing his fingers from Ray's hole.

At the last second, Mike replaced his fingers with the head of his cock, glorying in Ray's answering groan. He suddenly wished they were at Ray's apartment, in a soft bed that would make it possible for him to look Ray in the eyes as they fucked. Mike rocked his hips back and forth until his cock was fully buried inside Ray.

It only took one thrust for Mike to realise the hammer attached to the tool belt was a danger to Ray as it swung out and struck his hip.

"Ouch!"

"Shit, I'm sorry." Mike unfastened the buckle on the tool belt and dropped it to the ground. He rubbed Ray's reddened skin. "Are you okay?"

"I'm fine. It's all part of the experience, I guess."

Without breaking his rhythm, Mike chuckled. "I'll make sure to empty the damn thing entirely next time."

Ray turned his head around and met Mike's gaze. "It might be a couple of months before I'm ready to play construction worker and boss again, so you'll have to stick around in order to keep your word."

Mike bit the inside of his cheek to keep from agreeing. It would be so easy to say yes to anything Ray asked of him. Instead of answering, Mike grinned and began to fuck Ray harder. He reached around to stroke Ray's rock hard cock, pleased with himself when he felt the pre-cum that coated the thick rod. "Mmm, someone's ready to come."

"I hope that someone is you, because I'm...beyond ready," Ray said with a gasp.

"Come for me," Mike growled with need.

Within moments, he felt the warmth of Ray's cum cover his hand before dripping to the cement below.

"Oh fuck!" Ray yelled.

Mike released Ray's cock and wrapped a protective arm around Ray's stomach to steady him as his climax rocketed through him. Mike buried his cock as deep inside Ray as it would go and rode out his own orgasm, while trying to keep them both on their feet.

Strength waning, Mike lowered them to the ground, pulling Ray against his chest. "Wish I'd have thought of an air mattress. I could use a nap."

"Mmm hmm," Ray agreed, turning to snuggle deeper into Mike's embrace.

* * * *

Friday afternoon, Ray stopped by the construction site to check on the progress. He was amazed at how fast a building went up after the foundation was in. The exterior walls had been up for a couple of days but still no windows and the stacked stone had yet to be attached to the façade of the building.

Entering the two-story structure, Ray heard Mike's voice before he managed to locate him. Mike had been right when he said Ray would always think of them two of them fucking when he entered the building. Ray's face heated as he thought of the wild night. Mike's deep laugh helped settle Ray's nerves. Damn. Mike had a way of making Ray feel better no matter the situation. He followed Mike's laughter to the pool area and was surprised to see him on the phone. By the broad smile on Mike's face, Ray didn't need to ask who was on the other end of the call.

Mike noticed him and waved him over.

Although Mike continually told Ray he had nothing to worry about as far as Sidney was concerned, Ray didn't buy it. He'd liked Sidney when he'd met him months earlier, but he didn't understand what it was about the skinny architect that drew the unquestioning love and devotion of both Nash and Mike.

"Okay, my date's here. I'll see you Monday." Mike hung up the phone and shoved it in his pocket.

Ray's breath froze in his chest. "Sidney's coming?"

"Huh? No, that was Cole, the artisan I told you about from Chicago. I'm bringing him down to get a feel for the space."

"Oh, the wood guy, okay." Ray tried to be good, but it was too damn hard to be in the same room with

Mike and not want to kiss him. There were workmen all around them and only a few knew Ray and Mike were seeing each other. "God I want to kiss you right now."

A mischievous twinkle lit Mike's eyes. "You wanna know what I'd like to do to you right now?"

Ray hoped the verbal foreplay he and Mike enjoyed would never get old. "Something along the same lines as what you did to me before?"

Mike nodded. "See that saw horse over there?"

Ray looked in the direction Mike pointed. "I see it."

"I'd like to bend you over it, strip you out of those dress pants and stick my tongue as far into your asshole as it'll go. Then I'd pull my cock out and fuck you until you begged me to stop." Through the entire sexy speech, Mike's expression was pleasant but not overly friendly. He could've been talking about the dimensions for the room for all anyone around them knew.

"Not possible. I doubt I'll ever get enough of your cock," Ray said, trying to mimic Mike's stance and calm demeanour.

With a quiet groan, Mike shook his head. "You're killin' me. I still have a lot of work to get to before your ex-father-in-law pays a visit in the morning."

Bringing himself back to the problems at hand, Ray held up his hands. "That's why I'm here. Put me to work."

Mike chuckled. "You're not really dressed for sweeping the floors, which is really what I need done."

"I got a bag in the car with my work clothes. I didn't want to presume you'd let me help and show up in them."

"Help? Hell, you can work day and night if you want, it's your baby." Mike nudged Ray towards the front of the building. "I'll walk you to your car."

"Good idea."

On the way, Mike had to stop several times to talk to his workers, but soon enough they were outside in the bright afternoon sunshine. "When are they installing the windows?" Ray asked.

"I think the installers are due here next Thursday. I wish they were already up, but the manufacturer is taking more time because of the privacy glass issue. Better to wait and make sure they're right than to rush into it."

"I parked behind the office," Ray pointed out.

"And did you do that on purpose?"

"Maybe." Ray waited until they were behind the trailer to attack Mike's mouth in a deep, sloppy kiss. He'd spent the entire morning trying to finalise a project for one of his marketing clients when all he really wanted was to be with Mike. It was getting harder and harder to be away from the man he was quickly becoming attached to.

When a horn honked, Ray and Mike separated. Although they were hidden from the construction site, they were still in full view of passing traffic. "What am I going to do if Brock convinces Brent to pull the plug on the project?"

"I don't know, babe." Mike rested his hand on the small of Ray's back as they leaned against the side of Ray's car. "The smartest thing would be to buy Brent's half of the business and continue without him."

"I completely agree with you. Unfortunately, I can't get financial backing for that without him." Ray had run out of people to ask and the banks no longer cared to discuss it with him.

"We'll figure it out." Despite the traffic, Mike leaned in for another kiss. "You do set fire to my blood," he said, pulling out of the kiss.

Ray's blood was pretty damn heated as well. "Maybe it would be better if I ran inside and changed without you. We've both got a lot to get done before we can call it quits for the night."

"Are you trying to ruin my mood?" Mike gave Ray's ass a playful swat.

"Not at all. I'm trying to motivate you so we can get out of here early enough to grab a late dinner and still have enough energy to try that tongue thing you were talking about earlier."

"In that case, get your ass inside and change while I go crack the whip on Franco and his men."

* * * *

Ray was in the process of dumping another load of dirt and debris into the dumpster when his phone rang. When he glanced at the display, his heart sank. *Shit.* "Hey, Mom," he answered.

"Dad fell down the stairs and broke his leg. He's at North Kansas City Hospital and I need you to drive me there right now."

"Jesus! Did it just happen?"

"No, but he's due to be released today and the car's out of gas."

"Sorry to hear that, but can't he take a cab?" Ray may be cold where his parents were concerned, but he was only following their lead. He hadn't spoken to either of them in nearly a year and it wasn't by his decision.

"I don't have any money. Your father has his wallet with him, but he told me to come and get him. For

God's sake, Raymond, I'm simply asking you to put the past behind you and do what's right."

Ray dusted off his hands and carried the trashcan back inside the building. "I'm really busy right now. Can't it wait for another hour or so?" He refused to be pressured into jumping just because his father yelled; he'd done that his entire adolescence. Ray's mom was the queen at playing the guilt card, fortunately for Ray, it no longer worked. "I'll finish up and swing by to pick you up, but don't expect me to come inside."

"Fine." His mother ended the call without another word.

Ray shoved the phone into his pocket. He found Mike helping the rough-in crew on the second floor. "I need to talk to you."

Mike handed the two by four to one of the guys before joining Ray on the opposite side of the room. "What's up?"

"I need to go pick my dad up at the hospital and take him home," Ray explained. "You mind if I borrow your truck?"

"Your dad? He lives here? Why didn't I know that?"

"Because I don't talk about them, believe me, it's better that way. The one and only thing of use that my mom taught me was the old saying, if you don't have something nice to say, don't say anything at all." Ray shrugged. "So, I don't talk about 'em."

Mike handed Ray his keys. "You taking off now?"

"No. I'm gonna finish sweeping downstairs before I head out. I just wanted you to know."

"You want me to come with you?" Mike's expression was one of genuine concern.

"Thanks but it's not necessary. My dad doesn't have the power to hurt me anymore. I'm simply doing a favour for my mom so she'll leave me alone for another year." Ray knew he sounded bitter, but his relationship with his parents had never been more than distant. He had been a mistake that his mother had hidden from his father until too late to do anything about, and his father never once let him forget it.

"Call me if you need me."

"I shouldn't be gone long, two hours, tops." Ray went back to work, more concerned with Brock's inspection in the morning than anything else.

* * * *

Ray pulled into his parents' driveway and honked the horn. Two minutes later, his mother, Susan, came out of the house. Her pencilled in eyebrows drew together when she opened the door to the dusty pickup.

"What in heaven's name are you driving? We'd better swing by the car wash on the way or your father will have a fit."

"I borrowed my partner's truck, and no, I won't be going by the carwash." Ray realised it was the first time he'd referred to Mike as his partner. He wondered if it was too soon to even think of Mike in that fashion. Would it hurt more when Mike finished the job and went back to Chicago?

Ray waited for his mom to fasten her seat belt before backing out of the drive. "Yard looks nice," he said, searching for something to say.

"We hired a new service," Susan explained, wiping dust off the dashboard. "Is this friend of yours a farmer or something?"

"No, Mike owns the construction company we hired to build the athletic club."

Susan settled her purse in her lap. "Are you still talking about that crazy plan in this economy?"

"It's not a plan, Mom, we're really doing it. The club should be finished by late summer or early fall."

"Did you happen to see the news this morning?" Susan asked.

"No." It said a lot that his mother didn't inquire further into the status of the club, or that she didn't realise he'd said Mike was his partner. Although to be fair, his parents had only met Brent twice in all the years they'd been together, again, not his choice.

"The new Kauffman Center for Performing Arts is due to open in October. They had some pictures of it. Now that's quite a building."

"Yeah, I drive by it all the time. It's nice." The rest of the drive was relatively quiet, something Ray appreciated. It gave him time to think about the club and what he'd do if he lost it. He wondered if he could sell the land even though technically, Brent owned the majority of the building. In the beginning, Ray thought it was a good idea for them to each own a part of the business, that way they would always need each other. Of course that was several years ago when Ray had been desperate to hold onto Brent any way he could. In reality, the mess he currently found himself in was no one's fault but his own. He should've known better.

"I don't know why you hate your father and me so much, but I hope you at least try to get along with him when we get to the hospital," his mother said out of nowhere.

"I don't hate either of you," he replied in all honesty. "I just figured out a long time ago that it hurt a lot less to be indifferent towards you."

"What's that supposed to mean?"

"Nothing, Mom."

"Well you said it, so it has to mean something to you," she argued, her loud voice filling the inside of the cab.

There, that was the mother he remembered from his childhood, always screaming at him, always unhappy with her own life, and more than happy to take it out on her only child. Ray stopped in front of the hospital entrance. "I'm going to let you out here. I'll cruise the parking lot until you come back out with Dad."

"Do us both a favour and use the time to get this truck washed," Susan said before slamming the door.

Ray pulled out and headed towards the nearest car wash, not because he was afraid of his dad, but because the less he had to listen to his dad's voice, the better.

* * * *

Mike was taking a break when Ray walked in. The poor man looked dead on his feet. "That bad?"

Ray returned Mike's keys and sat beside him on the temporary staircase. "Worse. I washed your truck, by the way."

"You didn't have to do that."

"Yeah I did." Ray glanced around. "Everybody gone?"

"Everyone except Franco." Mike wrapped an arm around Ray's shoulders and drew his head over to rest against him. "You look beat."

"I'll be okay." Ray leaned further against Mike.

The obvious unease between Ray and his family bothered Mike. Not because he blamed either party, hell, he didn't know enough about the situation to make a call like that. He simply hated seeing Ray so distressed. Mike had lost his own dad years earlier when a fatal heart attack had taken the hero of the family too early. There were times when he thought he'd give anything to have one last talk with his dad, but Mike was wise enough to know that not every man was as fine a man as his dad.

"Let's get out of here. Right now I don't give a fuck what Brock says tomorrow," Ray mumbled.

Mike knew Ray didn't mean it, he'd been pushing himself too hard lately and it was starting to catch up with him. "I'll find Franco and tell him to knock off for the night." Mike kissed the side of Ray's head. "Wait here and I'll be back to drive you home."

After catching up with Franco, Mike led Ray outside and to his truck. "Looks pretty," he commented as he opened the door. "I'd almost forgotten what colour it was."

Ray smiled and climbed in.

Before Mike could open his door his phone rang. "What's up, trouble?" he asked his baby brother, Ben.

"Nash's had another heart attack, and this one's bad," Ben informed Mike.

Mike braced his hand against the side of the truck. "How bad?"

"Don't know yet. Right now it's touch and go. I'm working on your electrical schematics, but no one but you knows that building as well as Sidney. I just thought I'd give you a heads-up before I send these out tomorrow and also in case Sidney reaches out to you."

"He won't." The admission hurt but at the same time, it was incredibly freeing. Sidney's partner had suffered heart attacks before and never once had Sidney contacted him, despite the fact that he knew Mike loved him. "Keep me in the loop."

"Will do."

Mike pocketed the phone before getting into the truck. "That was Ben, Nash's had a serious heart attack, they're not sure he'll make it."

"Do you need to go back to Chicago?"

Mike reached across the seat and brushed Ray's cheek with the back of his hand. "No. Sidney has a lot of friends that'll take care of him." He gave Ray the best smile he could muster. "Besides, I've got a man right here who needs me."

Ray nodded. "I do."

Mike started the truck. It felt good to be needed, especially when it was by someone as fantastic as Ray. Sidney had his life, his friends and the man he loved above all others, it was about time Mike found the same. An idea suddenly came to mind. "Would you be interested in going home with me next weekend?"

"Why do I get the feeling you're not talking about your hotel?"

"Because you're a smart man. I'd like to introduce you to my family."

"I'll think about it," Ray answered, turning to stare out the passenger window.

Mike drove off-site, wondering if he'd overstepped with the request. "You don't have to if you don't want to."

"It's not that."

"Then what is it?" Mike headed towards Ray's apartment, figuring they could call and have something delivered for dinner.

"Do you really want me to meet your family or is this an excuse to see Sidney?"

Mike groaned. He knew why Ray had asked the question and he didn't blame him. "I'm not going to lie and say I won't see Sidney while we're there, but I hadn't planned to actively seek him out. I was telling you the truth when I told you Sidney had people closer to him that he would lean on at a time like this."

"So why suddenly do you want me to go to Chicago with you?"

"Hang on, I'll answer that question in a few minutes." Mike waited until he pulled into the parking garage of Ray's building. He turned off the engine and unfastened his seat belt. Turning to face Ray, Mike tugged on his arm until Ray scooted closer. Mike took Ray's face between his hands and brushed their lips together in a soft kiss. "I'm falling in love with you." He stopped himself and took a deep breath. "No, I'm not falling, I *am* in love with you, have been for a while now, but I've been too chicken to admit it."

"I feel the same way, but I've been trying to talk myself out of it."

Wow, that stung. "Gee, thanks."

"What do you want me to say? Your life's in Chicago and mine is here, and I don't want to give up mine any more than you do yours. So, where does that leave us, doing a long-distance relationship for the next twenty years? Do you honestly think that'll work?"

Mike had given their situation a lot of thought. He couldn't imagine moving away from his family and friends, but he didn't discount the possibility. Although it seemed Ray had. "If things go smoothly with Brock tomorrow, I'll still be here for another couple of months. And, since I don't see my feelings lessening over that period of time, what do you say we make decisions then."

"In other words, we should enjoy our time together and worry about the how when it happens."

"Yeah, something like that. The important thing is to introduce you to my family. We're all really close, and I'd like them to get to know you."

Ray wrinkled his nose. "What if they don't like me?"

Mike laughed. "Hell, if they liked Shane, they'll love you."

"Shane, your ex?"

Mike nodded. He'd told Ray about his only real long-term relationship soon after they'd started dating. "My brothers and sisters-in-law knew I wasn't truly in love, but they always treated Shane like a member of the family anyway. I know they'll see the difference in me now, because I'm happier than I've ever been."

"I'll go, but I can't promise how I'll react if I see Sidney."

"In all honesty, you'll probably feel like I feel when Brent comes around." Mike squeezed Ray's hand. "It's okay."

"The situation is completely different," Ray argued.

"Yeah, because I've never fucked Sidney. Every time I see Brent, I picture him under you and it drives me crazy."

"But I left Brent, and in a way, Sidney left you. There's a difference."

"Sidney didn't leave me, hell, I never had a chance with him. You know, I've realised something lately. I think I loved who Sidney is as a person more because he was so unwavering in his loyalty to Nash. It's a characteristic you don't find much these days. I knew I wanted that kind of loyalty directed towards me, so I made up an imaginary relationship in my head between the two of us and allowed it to become an obsession." He leaned in and gave Ray a kiss.

"Because of you, I know what the real thing feels like, and I'm not about to do anything to jeopardise that."

"Then you have to stop feeling jealous around Brent, because you'll never again find him under me. I've always wanted the same thing you're talking about, and I'm not stupid enough to fall for Brent again or anyone else for that matter, not if I have you."

Mike knew he'd continue to feel uneasy around Brent, it was his nature. Brent was a lot younger and prettier than him and he knew it, and as Mike had seen first-hand, when Brent wanted something, he wasn't shy about going after it. Still, his issues with Brent were his own, and he did trust Ray. "As long as we're on the same page," he replied, knowing Ray expected some kind of response.

Chapter Five

Upon meeting Brock Atwood, Mike knew immediately why Ray found the man so off-putting. Arrogance oozed off the older businessman as he stepped out of the black stretch limousine. *Who the hell hires a limo to take them to a construction site?* He glanced at Ray and rolled his eyes. "What a tool," he whispered under his breath as Brock stalked towards the building.

"Where's Brent?" Ray asked, catching up with Brock.

"Still in bed, I assume. My son jumps into things with his heart instead of his brain. I'm here to make sure you're not taking advantage of that particular personality flaw."

At the statement, Ray stopped and squared his shoulders. Suddenly he went from nervous ex-lover to business investor. "I can assure you that the athletic club is a sound investment. Moreover, I, myself, wouldn't have let it get to this stage if I thought the idea was foolish. Please don't forget that Brent's money isn't the only resource we're using for this project. The real estate you're currently standing on didn't come cheap, and I paid for that on my own."

Mike stood back, impressed beyond measure with the man he loved.

"That may be, but throwing good money after bad will bankrupt a person in no time." Brock walked into the building. "Seems awfully large," he commented, looking around. "A bit excessive, don't you think? Brent said you told him to cap the membership at five hundred. From what I see, you could fit a hell of a lot more people in here than that. It just doesn't make sense. You should either scale down the project or up the membership. Anything else is asking for trouble."

"You belong to a country club, do you not?" Ray asked Brock.

"You know I do."

"Why do you belong to the country club instead of playing tennis on the community courts or shooting a round of golf at one of the local courses? It's all about exclusivity, that's what people pay for. Brookside Athletic Club is no different than your fifty some odd acre country club. Our members will be the people who can pay on time at the price we set, or we'll drop them and bring someone else in who can, and they know it." Ray produced a leather binder from the briefcase he carried. "I ask you to please take a look at this business plan that I've created. Give it a fair perusal, and I believe you'll find I've done my homework."

By the time Ray handed over the portfolio, Mike was speechless. No wonder Ray felt so passionately about the project. He really had done his homework. Hell, Mike was ready to cash in his stocks and give Ray the money he needed. The thought struck him unexpectedly. He'd never considered becoming a partner in the club, but by the end of Ray's sales pitch, Mike was definitely intrigued by the idea and he knew nothing about the athletic club business.

"If you advise Brent to pull out of the project, I'll step in," Mike declared. "One way or another, this club will be finished. Brent can either hook his wagon to the gravy train or lose out on a lot of money. If I were you, I'd be careful to make the right decision."

Ray's jaw dropped at Mike's offer. "You mean it?" he asked, turning his back on Brock.

"Yeah, I do. I may not have the financial clout Brent does, but I have enough to convince the bank to let me step in." Mike was shocked he'd made the offer without consulting his brothers, but if it came to it, he could do it without them.

Brock held up the leather binder Ray had given him. "Let me talk to Brent, and have my accountant go over the numbers. I'll get back to you in a couple of days."

"You'll have until Wednesday at noon," Ray announced. "I'll be heading out of town for a long weekend on Friday, and I'd like to get things settled before I leave."

Brock nodded and started to walk out of the building, but Ray stopped him. "On a personal level, I need you to know something. Despite what you always thought of me, I loved your son. We both tried to make it work, but in the end, we wanted different things. That being said, if Brent still wants to be part of the club, I'm agreeable to that. We can continue with the same plans for the business that we discussed before we parted company."

"I'll talk to him." Brock glanced from Ray to Mike and back to Ray. "I must say, you do have a gift when it comes to getting men to hand over their money. As a businessman, I appreciate the quality, but as a father, it unnerves me."

Ray jerked as if he'd been struck by a physical blow, but said nothing in return. The moment Brock walked out of the building, he turned his attention to Mike. "Why'd you do that?"

"Do what, offer to save the club if Brock passes? Because I may get dirty and tromp around a construction site for a living, but I know a good investment when I hear it." Even if Mike had to put up his house as collateral, it would still be a wise investment. The fact that a business partnership with Ray would keep them connected and keep Brent out of the picture was a pure bonus.

"My only concern is that you'll do it because you want to and not because of me. Brock was right in a way. Brent came up with the idea for the club, but I'm the one who took the ball and ran with it. Christ, Brent was always looking for ways to spend money, why I paid more attention to this one over the others is anyone's guess."

"Don't let what Brock said get to you. One way or another, the club will be built, so stop worrying about the past and plan for the future. We still have a lot to do before you can open the doors." Mike rested his hands on Ray's shoulders. "You can trust me on that."

"Okay, I will."

* * * *

With his head resting in Mike's lap, and Mike's hand casually fondling his cock, Ray was pulled away from his magazine by a knock on the door. With a groan, he let the magazine drop to the floor. He knew who his visitor was. He'd actually been expecting Brent since the meeting with Brock the previous day. "This'll probably go better if you watch the game in the bedroom."

Mike released Ray's cock and moved up to rub his stomach. "I'd rather stay if you don't mind."

The knock came again, only louder. Ray swung his legs over the side of the couch and stood, pulling his pyjama pants up around his waist. He bent and gave Mike a deep kiss. "I love you, but I really need to handle this on my own."

Mike studied Ray for a moment. "Fine, but if shit starts to get out of hand, I'm coming in."

"Okay," Ray agreed. He waited until Mike was out of the room before opening the door. "Hey."

Without being asked, Brent barged inside Ray's apartment. "What did you say to my father?"

Ray shut the door. "Nothing bad, I promise you. I explained the business model I'd worked on and gave him the portfolio. Isn't that what I was supposed to do?"

Brent made a show of looking Ray up and down. "Is he here?"

"That's none of your business. Now, get to the point or leave." Ray crossed his arms over his bare chest, wishing he had a shirt to put on.

"I still haven't decided whether or not I want to go forward with the club, but suddenly my dad is pushing me into it. Did you threaten him or something?"

"Of course not. Brock knows a good deal when he sees it. Evidently, you making money is more important to him than whether you're comfortable working with me or not. Either way, that's between the two of you. I did tell him he had until Wednesday to figure it out," Ray added.

"Why did you tell him that? This is between you and me."

"It was, until you brought him into it. I figured you'd do whatever he told you to do. That *is* why you asked him to come, right? And don't deny that you didn't ask him because I know you did."

"How do you know?"

"Because you've never been able to fight for yourself. You wanted a way out and you were hoping Brock would give it to you, but it backfired and now you're mad."

Brent stared at Ray. "You want me to back out, don't you? You have a lot of nerve. The night you walked out, you practically begged me to stay on. Now that *Mike's* in the picture you don't need me anymore."

Ray held his tongue, unable to deny the accusation. "I'll tell you one thing, if you decide to keep with the project; you'll have to get used to Mike being around, because if I have my way, we'll be together for a long time."

Brent snorted. "Yeah, until he goes back to Chicago."

"That's really none of your business." Ray grabbed the door handle. "Now, if you don't mind, I'd like to get back to enjoying my Sunday afternoon."

"Knowing you're with him is driving me crazy. Are you trying to get back at me? Because if I wanted to, I could make things very difficult for you."

"Are you threatening me?" Ray released the door handle and took a step towards Brent.

Brent held up his hands in surrender. "I'm just trying to make you understand that you can't pin all your hopes on that guy. Think about it, we were strong until he came along. Don't shut me out."

"Stop. I'm not getting into this with you again. I'm sorry, but you and I are over. I refuse to feel guilty because I've moved on when you seemed to have moved on while the two of us were still together." Finished with the conversation, he opened the door. "Think about the business, and I'll accept whatever you decide, but leave Mike out of it."

Brent stopped in the doorway. "Is he really that important to you?"

Knowing Mike was in the adjacent room, a sense of calm overcame Ray. "Yeah, he is."

"It might've worked between us if you'd fought for me like that," Brent mumbled.

"I did fight for you. Every time you brought another man into our bed, I had to fight for you." Ray shut the door without waiting for Brent's reply. He leaned his forehead against the door and locked it.

"You okay?" Mike asked, stepping up behind him.

"Yeah." Ray closed his eyes as Mike wrapped his arms around him. The safety Mike provided went deeper than anything Ray had experienced. In Mike's embrace, Ray was able to forget about his lonely upbringing and the shame brought on by sharing Brent with others. He was free to be himself and although he hadn't known Mike for long, he felt accepted for who he was. "Maybe I should just walk away from the club."

"That's not the answer and we both know it." Mike kissed Ray's neck. "Let's get back to our lazy Sunday."

Ray turned around and followed Mike. "The bedroom?" he questioned when Mike bypassed the couch.

"If you don't mind, I'd like to hold you for a while." Mike pushed his sweats down and kicked them to the corner of the room. They hadn't made the bed yet, knowing they'd get back to it before the day was over.

Mike climbed in and kicked all but the sheet to the bottom of the bed.

Ray shut the blinds, easing the room into darkness. "I thought you were going to turn on the game?" He removed his pyjama pants and scooted to the centre to drape himself over Mike.

After moving to lean his upper body against the headboard, Mike ran his fingers through Ray's hair. "That was your idea. Mine was to make sure Brent didn't try anything."

Ray reached for the remote and turned on the baseball game. "There." He settled back down with his head resting on Mike's lower stomach. It was the perfect position. If he tilted his head back, he could reach one of Mike's dark nipples with the tip of his tongue, and if he looked down he could watch Mike's cock harden as he fondled it.

Starting with Mike's chest, Ray laved a nipple while reaching under the sheet to brush his fingers lightly up the length of Mike's flaccid cock. Mike ran his hand down Ray's back as he continued to pretend to watch the game. "Is there anything I don't do for you that you'd like me to?"

"What're you talking about?"

"I want you to be satisfied." Ray leant back on his elbow and met Mike's gaze.

"Oh, I'm more than satisfied. My dick's never been so happy, and that's all you, babe." He tugged on Ray's arm until Ray moved to straddle Mike's lap. "Just because I don't fuck you every second of the day, don't ever think I don't want you. But I've learned the hard way that there's more to building a solid foundation than good sex."

Ray understood what Mike was saying because he felt the same way. "If there ever is anything, promise you'll tell me."

Mike cupped Ray's ass. "I'm not Brent. You don't have to worry about me looking for something different."

Brent's parting words the night he'd left continued to haunt Ray. So far he'd shied away from fucking Mike, afraid of making the same mistakes he'd made with Brent, but he needed to take the final leap of trust. "Let me make love to you."

Mike grinned. "I wondered when you were going to get around to asking."

"Is that a yes?"

"That's an absolutely."

Ray's hand shook as he reached to the bedside table for the bottle of lube and a condom. "God, I'm so nervous," he admitted.

Mike scooted down until his head rested on the pillow. "Why? You think I've never been fucked before?"

"Not by me."

Mike took the lube from Ray and pulled him down for a hug. "Let's just lie here a bit."

Ray settled into Mike's warm embrace, disappointed with himself. Damn Brent for giving him doubts. No matter how many times he told himself that Brent was merely trying to hurt him, Ray couldn't help but feel partially responsible for Brent's wandering ways.

"Your Royals suck," Mike commented, his attention returned to the game on TV.

"Yeah, but we like 'em anyway. After we won the World Series in the mid-eighties everyone said it would take a while to rebuild the team, well, it's been about twenty five years. I think the team could've been rebuilt several times over by now, but we keep hoping."

Mike kissed Ray's temple. "You love this town, don't you?"

"More than I should, probably. There's just something about the people here. I don't know how to explain it, but they're real, you know? Maybe it's because we're a well-kept secret, but even though there's a fairly large population, most people have a small town friendliness about them." Ray shut up before he said something to offend Mike. Nothing against Mike and his family, but Ray hadn't cared for Chicago the few times he'd visited. Walking in the city made him feel claustrophobic. It was the same when he'd travelled to New York City, too many people, too much traffic, way too many skyscrapers. He'd never understood the allure.

Ray yawned, the week finally catching up with him. He had another tough week ahead. He snuggled against Mike and reached down to pull the sheet over them. It was nice to be held without feeling he needed to perform. Rarely had he and Brent taken the time to lie together for the sake of spending time with each other. With Brent it was always the demand for sex instead of intimacy. Ray had found he enjoyed one as much as the other, it was further proof that he'd found the right man for him.

* * * *

"What a great spot," Cole said, pulling out his chair to sit.

Mike had grown fond of the Plaza and couldn't wait to share the unbelievable restaurants with one of his closest friends. "Yeah, I love this weather. It's perfect for outside dining." He sat across from Cole, leaving the chair beside him for Ray, who had stopped inside the restaurant to talk to someone he knew.

"I approve of your choice," Cole commented.

"I thought you'd like it. They make a fantastic pan seared chicken dish, loaded with garlic."

Cole chuckled. "I was talking about Ray."

"Oh." Mike glanced over his shoulder, barely able to make out Ray's silhouette within the dark interior of the restaurant. "He's quickly becoming everything to me." It was a bold admission for him. Rarely, if ever, did Mike talk about his sex life, especially around Cole. The six-foot-three artisan was well known around Boystown as a much sought after companion for the evening, and despite the fact Cole didn't do commitments, he had a line of men a mile long waiting to change his mind. "So stay away from him."

Cole held up his hands and laughed. "You know I wouldn't do that to you, although that waiter over there is a different story. Damn, they grow 'em sexy in Kansas City."

Ray appeared at the table, giving Mike's shoulder an affectionate squeeze before taking his seat. "Sorry about that. He's one of my clients."

"No problem." Cole took a sip of his drink. "What is it you do?"

"I'm a marketing consultant for independent restaurants. Actually, I do all the marketing for this place." Ray accepted the glass of wine from the waiter. "Thanks, Shawn."

Mike noticed the look that passed between Cole and Shawn before the waiter returned to his duties. He shook his head. "Jeez, Cole, you've only been in town two hours."

"Hey, I won't be here that long this time around. I need to make the most of it."

That was something else Mike intended to talk to Cole about. "The way I figure it, you'll need to be in town at least a month and a half, if not two. Is that going to be a problem? I can hire guys to stain the woodwork, but everything else will fall to you."

Cole rested his tanned forearms on the table. "I'll need at least one assistant to help with the staircase, preferably two, but I can make do with one. And I'll need someone familiar with relief work to clean up and sand out any of the rough edges on the carvings once I finish them."

Mike nodded. Cole usually created his masterpieces in his studio in Chicago, but when Mike had begged him to do the on-site pieces for the athletic club, Cole had agreed out of friendship. Of course he was being paid handsomely for his work, but money never seemed to be Cole's motivating factor. It had taken a few hours to convince Ray that quality woodwork in a building as massive as the club would make all the difference in the world in adding a rich, warm feeling to all who entered. "I'll see what I can find." Surely Franco knew of someone.

Shortly after Shawn came back to the table to take their orders, Mike's phone rang. "It's Ben. Excuse me for a minute." He excused himself.

Cole leaned towards Ray the moment Mike stepped away from the table. "Is this thing between you and Mike serious?"

Unsure of what Mike had already told Cole about their relationship, Ray wasn't sure how to answer. "I think so. Why?"

Cole grinned. "Just checking."

Ray's hackles rose. "Checking because you're interested in him, or checking to make sure I'm serious?"

Cole didn't appear to be phased by Ray's anger. "Both. You're good-looking, but I won't poach on someone he genuinely likes. He told me his side of things. I was making sure you felt the same way."

Although he didn't say it, Cole reminded Ray a lot of Brent. "I should introduce you to my ex. I think the two of you would get along."

"Ouch!" Cole finished his Scotch and water.

"Brent's an okay guy," Ray tried to clarify. "He simply doesn't believe in fucking the same person for the rest of his life."

Cole's eyes lit up. "You'll have to give me his number."

Ray was tempted to give Brent a call and pass the phone to Cole on the spot. If Brent was busy being distracted by Cole, he wouldn't have time to make trouble for Ray and Mike. "I'll definitely do that."

"Do what?" Mike asked, coming back to the table.

"Hook me up with his ex," Cole clarified.

Mike laughed. "You know I love you, Cole, but I don't think even you could keep up with Brent."

"I'd be more than willing to give it a try." Cole looked incredibly smug and Ray had no doubt both men would love the challenge the other presented.

* * * *

"Brent's on his way," Ray announced, finding Cole and Mike in the office.

Cole rubbed his hands together. "Finally."

Mike reached out and punched Cole in the arm. "Watch your mouth. This is business. We've been waiting to hear whether or not Brent wants to keep his half of the club or whether he's going to sell it to me."

"You? You don't know a damn thing about running a gym," Cole argued.

"You're right about that, but Ray's more than qualified to take care of the day to day stuff. I'll be more of a silent partner with *special* benefits."

Ray felt his face flush at the announcement. He cleared his throat and told Mike with a dirty look that he didn't appreciate the comment.

"Sorry, babe." Mike leaned over and kissed Ray, keeping the tongue-play to a minimum for Cole's benefit. "You want to talk to Brent alone or would you rather I stay?"

"Alone would probably be better." Ray glanced at Cole when he made a noise deep in his throat. "Don't worry, I told you I'd introduce the two of you and I will."

"Excellent." Cole headed to the door. "Come on, Mike, let's go drool over Franco some more."

Mike scowled at Cole before turning back to Ray. "I swear, I have *never* drooled over Franco."

Ray thought of the combative relationship between Franco and Mike when they'd first started working together. "Don't worry, I believe you."

Instead of waiting inside, Ray decided he'd rather have the conversation outside. He stood beside the trailer in a shady spot and waited for Brent.

A short time later, Brent pulled up and got out of the car. "Hey," Brent greeted.

"Your folks gone?" Ray asked.

"They went home Sunday. Mom finally put her foot down and told Dad to butt out of my business."

"That's good, right?" Ray wasn't sure anymore where Brent stood on the partnership.

"I guess. Unfortunately, I didn't have anyone else to talk to about the decision in front of me."

"You've got friends," Ray reminded his ex.

"Not friends I trust to give me decent advice." Brent smiled for the first time in weeks.

Ray realised how much he missed it. Maybe the break-up had affected Brent more than Ray thought it would. "Were you able to come to a decision?"

Brent stuck his hands in the deep pockets of his cargo shorts. "I'd like to try. If it doesn't work between us, I'll agree to sell my half to Mike or whoever else you might be with at the time, but for now, I still want it."

Ray wasn't sure if the bit about Mike was meant as a jab or if Brent honestly didn't understand how deeply Ray felt for Mike. "Okay. We'll have to sit down and iron out a few things, like who will be in charge of what, but I'm willing to try."

"Will Mike give me shit for this?" Brent asked.

"I don't think so. Mike just wants me to be happy." Ray refused to believe otherwise.

"Good." Brent looked towards the building. The stacked stone façade was going up, a detail that completely transformed the outside of the building. "There's a lot done since the last time I was here."

"Yeah," Ray agreed. "Come on, I'll show you around. There's someone I'd like to introduce you to, anyway."

"Cool."

While a part of Ray was glad he'd managed to salvage at least a working partnership with Brent, he couldn't help but wonder what the decision would mean in terms of his relationship with Mike. If Mike didn't buy in then he'd have no reason to relocate to Kansas City. Hell, for that matter, Mike wouldn't even have a reason to visit other than trying to make a long-distance relationship work. Ray began to worry he wouldn't be enough.

Chapter Six

It felt strange for Mike to drive around in a rented car, but it was good to be home. "I thought we'd run to my place and get cleaned up before meeting my family for dinner. Mom already had plans, but she'll meet us at Steven's after dinner."

Ray turned away from the view out his side window and glanced at Mike. "Sounds good. Why did I think you lived in Chicago?"

"Technically, I live in Winnetka, but it's easier to tell people Chicago because unless you're from here, you don't know where the hell Winnetka is."

"It's pretty," Ray mumbled.

The small village of Winnetka was in fact pretty, or so Mike had always believed. He hadn't grown up there, but it was one of those places he'd always dreamed of buying a house. When a lot at the edge of town became available, Mike snapped it up without even bothering to try to bargain for a cheaper price. "This is me." He pulled into the long blacktop driveway in front of the stone and timber house of his dreams.

"It looks a lot like the athletic club," Ray noted.

"It should. Sidney designed it. One of his first projects when he started working for my brother, Ben." Mike didn't elaborate, knowing Sidney was a touchy subject as far as Ray was concerned. He got out of the car and opened the trunk to retrieve their luggage.

"It really is stunning." Ray took his weekend bag and stood beside the car. "You get a lot of snow though, right?"

Mike nodded, still trying to get a feel for Ray's mood. "I'd say it's the one downside, but I'm used to it, so most of the time I deal with it as it comes." He led the way up the front walk and unlocked the door, gesturing for Ray to precede him. "Bedroom's in the back."

Ray tore his gaze away from the soaring stone fireplace. "I'll follow you."

Mike walked through the open-style living room and kitchen to the hallway that led to the master suite and media room. He tossed the small bag onto the floor and collapsed on the bed. Staring up at Ray, he held out his arms. "Come join me."

Ray set his suitcase down before sitting on the edge of the bed. "This place fits you."

Mike pulled Ray down and into his arms. "What's going on?"

Ray shrugged. "I guess I didn't give enough thought to your life here. For some reason, I pictured you living in an apartment downtown." He rolled his eyes. "Okay, the truth is, I imagined you working all day on a construction site before going home to a tiny little apartment in a bad part of town."

"I'm part owner of a well-known construction company. Why in the world would you picture me in a dingy apartment?" Mike wondered if it had something to do with his vocation. It wasn't the first time someone had taken him at face value. He may not talk or act like he had money, but that was an attribute as far as Mike was concerned. There was nothing he hated more than people who flaunted their wealth.

"I don't know. I guess to make myself feel better." Ray rolled on top of Mike. "I'm sorry. It doesn't matter."

Mike rubbed Ray's back. "I'm still the same man you've always known. Don't let the fancy digs fool you."

Ray grinned. "How much time do we have before we have to leave?"

"We're meeting in an hour, but it'll only take about ten minutes or so to get there. Why, what did you have in mind?"

Ray climbed off Mike and began to unbutton his shirt. "Shower?"

Mike's cock immediately became interested. "That's exactly what I was hoping you'd say." He pulled his sports shirt over his head and tossed it to the floor.

Within a matter of minutes, they were both naked and standing under the hot spray of the oversized shower. Mike set the supplies on the wide bench and turned his attention to Ray. He'd told Ray before how he felt, but he was beginning to doubt whether or not Ray truly believed him. Ray's obvious distress over Mike's living situation was a problem. "Do you have any idea how deeply I've fallen in love with you?"

Instead of answering, Ray poured liquid soap into his palm and began to wash Mike's chest.

"Did you hear me?" Mike wrapped his hands around Ray's wrists to still them. It wasn't that he didn't like Ray's attention, he liked it a little too much, and they needed to get a few things settled between them before they met his family for dinner.

"I don't know what to say. I see this town and this house, and I know in my heart you'll never give it up."

Mike released Ray's wrist and pulled him into a hug. At least he knew the truth, but maybe it was time he told Ray why they were in town. "I plan to talk to my brothers about opening an arm of Shrivers' Construction in Kansas City when we meet them."

Ray pushed against Mike's chest. "Are you serious?"

"Let me back up. Do you have any idea how deeply I've fallen in love with you?" Mike repeated his earlier proclamation.

Ray began to move his head up and down in slow motion. "I think I'm starting to, but I don't understand why you'd willingly leave all this. Your family's here, your business…" Ray held up his arms. "This house is fucking awesome. I can't compare to this."

"You're right." Mike smiled when Ray's expression fell. "But none of it means anything without someone to share it with. My family will never stop loving me just because I move to Kansas City, but you might if I don't, and I simply refuse to take that chance."

"No one's ever loved me like you do. And I'm afraid I'll let you down."

Mike leant forward and kissed Ray hard, nicking his bottom lip in the process, but it was worth it if it would shake Ray up. "Dammit, Ray, stop doubting yourself. Brent fucked up, but that's his problem. He's the one who'll wake up one day and realise he let the finest man in the world slip through his fingers. I'm not him, and I'm not that stupid."

Ray grabbed the bottle of soap and poured a generous amount down the front of Mike's chest. "I'm glad I found a smart man to love." He began to run his fingers through Mike's chest hair, building lather as he went.

"I'm pretty dirty a little lower, in case you're interested." Mike braced his hand against the tile wall.

"You mean here?" Ray slid his hands down Mike's groin.

Mike spread his legs. "You're close."

"Hmmm." Ray soaped Mike's balls, easing his way to Mike's ass. He swirled his finger around the puckered hole, and Mike thought he'd melt with the pleasure.

Groaning, he lifted his right leg and rested his foot on the built-in bench. He hoped to hell Ray wasn't starting something he didn't plan to finish. It had been ages since Mike had felt the slow burn of a cock sliding in and out of his ass. In need of more, Mike changed positions, moving to lean over the bench, his ass sticking proudly out for more of Ray's special attention.

Ray didn't miss a beat, kneeling behind Mike. With each touch of Ray's tongue against his hole Mike moaned, a begging plea at the tip of his tongue. Time was quickly ticking away, and Mike wasn't sure if he could honestly lie to his brothers and their wives about the reason they were late. "Fuck me."

Ray placed kisses on Mike's back as he reached for the bottle of lube. When the container slipped from Ray's grasp, Mike retrieved it and handed it back. "Sorry," Ray mumbled.

Mike could hear the slight shake to Ray's voice and knew his partner was nervous. When Ray's slick finger circled Mike's hole, they both seemed to hold their breath. A finger entered Mike, filling him almost immediately. He bit the inside of his cheek at the pinch of pain, hoping his body didn't tense.

"Okay?"

"I will be as soon as you add another." It was a small lie, but he needed to help build Ray's confidence.

Ray chuckled. "Hang on."

Mike felt the shower shut off before another slicked finger began to saw in and out of him in expert rhythm. "So good," Mike encouraged. Despite Ray's nerves, it was obvious the man knew how to fuck, but of course he did. He'd been fucking Brent for years. Mike squeezed his eyes shut, trying to block out any memory of Ray having another man in his life.

Mike reached for the condom and tore the wrapper open. "Now," he urged, holding the rubber behind him.

"You're not stretched enough," Ray argued, scissoring his fingers.

"Yeah I am." All Mike wanted was to feel Ray's length inside him.

Ray pressed the sheathed tip of his cock against Mike's semi-stretched hole and slowly rocked his way inside. With each inch, Mike's grip on the bench tightened, not out of pain, but an undeniable pleasure.

"Oh my God, why did we wait so long for this?" Mike asked without thinking.

Buried to the hilt, Ray pulled out before sliding back inside. "I think that's about to change."

"I hope so." Mike rocked back to meet Ray's thrusts. As good as his ass felt, Mike almost came unhinged when Ray reached under him and wrapped a hand around his cock. "Ahh, fuuuckk," he cried, his voice echoing off the tiled walls.

Ray's firm grip on Mike's cock was just the right amount of pressure combined with the slide of his cock against Mike's prostate on each thrust. It was obvious to Mike that whatever doubts Ray had about his skills in the bedroom, they were completely unfounded. He slapped his palm against the bench in an attempt to control his climax. A moment later, Mike came, his seed spilling over Ray's fist. Unable to form a coherent thought, Mike let out a loud growl as his body tensed with the force of his orgasm.

"Yeah," Ray shouted. He released Mike's cock and gripped his shoulders as he buried his dick as deep as possible. With a loud grunt, Ray pistoned his hips once more and came.

By the time Ray collapsed against Mike's back, Mike's legs were shaking. He eased them both to the floor of the shower and leaned his head against the teak bench. "Christ, how could you've ever doubted yourself," he panted.

Ray answered with another grunt, still resting his cheek against Mike's back. "Your ass is a hell of a lot tighter than Brent's." Out of nowhere, Ray started to chuckle. "Guess that shouldn't come as a surprise, huh?"

"You said it, not me."

* * * *

Ray sat back while the Shriver brothers shared insults and stories of their youth. It was a scene he wasn't used to, and wasn't immediately sure how to take their relationship. Rhonda, Mike's older brother Steven's wife, leaned closer to Ray. "I know it's irritating, but you'll get used to it. You'd never know how much they love each other. Maybe it's a brother thing."

"Maybe," Ray agreed. "I was an only child."

Rhonda pointed towards herself. "Sisters."

Mike lifted his wine glass and smiled affectionately at his family. "Although you've busted my chops all evening, it's good to be home."

Ray followed the customary tradition and clinked his glass against all those he could reach. He plastered on a fake smile, hoping no one would notice the way the toast actually made him feel. Despite Mike's earlier declaration of moving to Kansas City, something inside Ray told him he couldn't let it happen.

"The reason I wanted you all here tonight was to share with you my plans for the future," Mike began.

Ray quickly reached over and squeezed Mike's thigh in an attempt to get his attention. Mike glanced at Ray with a questioning expression. Ray shook his head. "Don't," he whispered.

Mike set his glass down. "Excuse us for a minute." He stood and pulled Ray up beside him. "Can I speak to you in private?"

"Sorry," Ray apologised to the others at the table. He followed Mike through the restaurant until they stood outside on the sidewalk.

"What's going on?" Mike rested his hands on Ray's shoulders.

"I can't let you do this." Unable to break away without force, Ray closed his eyes in an attempt to hide from Mike's angry gaze.

"What're you talking about? Have you changed your mind about us?"

"No." Ray opened his eyes to get his point across. "You have too much to lose to just pick up and leave. I guess I didn't realise that until tonight." Ray knew what the solution to their problem was, but he wasn't ready to admit it, even to himself. "Give them a chance to get to know me, please. I don't want them to hate me because I'm taking you away from them. I've never had a family, but I'm starting to see what a real one looks like. I'd like to be a part of that if it's okay?"

Mike pulled Ray into a hug. "Is that what you're worried about? Oh, babe, they're going to fall in love with you like I did. Moving won't change their feelings, I promise."

"You don't know that, and I'm not ready to take the chance. Let's wait," he begged. "If you really believe we have a future together, we have time."

Mike released his hold on Ray and stepped back. "I'll wait until you feel more comfortable as long as you tell me this isn't your way of trying to put distance between us."

"That's the last thing I want." Building a future with Mike and his family meant everything, and that was the problem. Ray needed to think.

"Okay. I'll save the announcement, but you do realise it'll take time to set up a new arm of the company, right?"

"I understand."

* * * *

After dinner, they moved the welcome home gathering to Steven's house to wait for their mother to arrive. Designed for big family gatherings, the house was perfect. While Rhonda gave Ray a tour, Mike joined his brothers in the kitchen for a beer.

"I take it things have gotten serious between you two." Ben handed Mike a beer.

"Yeah." The best thing about Mike's brothers was their accepting attitude towards his homosexuality. He wanted to tell his brothers he loved Ray so much he was willing to move to be with him, but Ray's earlier plea stopped him.

"Is it different than what you felt for Shane?" Jamie, Mike's youngest brother, asked.

Mike still wasn't proud of the way he'd led Shane on for five years, hoping he'd fall in love. "Very different. Thanks for bringing Shane into the conversation, by the way." He reached out and flicked Jamie on the back of the head.

Jamie reacted predictably and punched Mike in the shoulder. "Hey, it's not my fault you're being all mysterious where Ray's concerned. What was up with that suck-ass toast earlier anyway?"

"I started to tell you guys how I felt about him, but he wasn't comfortable with it. He wants to give you all a chance to get to know him first." Mike refused to lie to his family, but he wouldn't break his promise to Ray either. Hopefully his brothers would let the subject drop. "So, how's business? Anything big lined up?" he asked Steven.

"I was hoping you'd ask. We've been approached by a group of investors who'd like us to design and build a new office complex in Libertyville. I'd like to put in a bid, but I can't do it unless you think you'll be done in Kansas City before late fall."

Mike shifted his stance, uncomfortable with the situation. "I can give you the name of a couple guys I think could head up a project like that just in case we're not done with the KC job in time." He couldn't commit to the project, but he didn't want Shrivers' Construction to pass it up either.

"Is everything on schedule?" Steven rinsed his bottle and tossed it into the recycling bin hidden beneath the island.

"So far, but we've barely started on the inside, so a number of things could delay us. Cole was in last week to look over the building. We should be ready for him in another month or so."

Again, trying to turn the conversation away from himself, Mike looked at Ben. "Have you heard from Sidney lately?"

"Yeah, I told him to take as much time as he needed. He said he'd try to get some things done from home though, so that should help."

"But Nash is doing better, right?" He received regular updates and had spoken with Sidney on the phone several days ago, but Sidney was always so damn optimistic, Mike wasn't sure whether or not he was getting the full story.

Ben sighed. "For now, but like Dad, you never really know when that fatal blow is going to happen. I think Sidney's trying to remain positive, but surely he knows Nash's already living on borrowed time."

"I'm sure if Sidney has anything to do with it, Nash'll be his old self in no time. Nash has too much to live for to give up without a fight." Mike was pleased he felt so at peace with his feelings for Sidney. No longer did he get butterflies in his stomach when he saw, spoke or thought of Sidney. It was a direct testament to how much he loved Ray. He knew he no longer needed the fantasy Sidney provided to get through the day. Now that he had a man to love and love him in return, he could understand why Sidney had never even considered cheating on Nash. Mike couldn't imagine anyone else filling his heart the way

Ray had. Taking the job in Kansas City had been the best decision of his life.

* * * *

After finishing the tour, Ray went in search of Mike. Rhonda told him the men often enjoyed sitting around the kitchen island, swapping stories, so that's where Ray headed. Before he entered the room, he heard Steven ask Mike about starting another job in Chicago. Ray held his breath, wondering if Mike would tell his brothers of his plan to relocate to Kansas City.

It was obvious from Mike's answer that he was uncomfortable. *Damn.* The last thing Ray wanted was to cause trouble for Mike. He caught a glimpse of the brothers in the reflection of a mirror hanging on the wall in the breakfast area. The scene warmed him. It would be impossible for anyone not to see the resemblance between the men. Ray had often wondered what it would be like to have a sibling. Did he have the right to ask Mike to move away from them?

When the subject of Sidney came up, Ray's stomach began to roil. Mike's statement about Sidney actually made Ray feel better. He detected concern in Mike's voice but not the love he'd heard the first time Mike had told him about Sidney.

The ringing doorbell made Ray jump, reminding him that he'd been eavesdropping. He cleared his throat and stepped into the kitchen. "Hey."

Mike stood and grabbed Ray's hand on his way out of the room. "Let's go introduce you to Mom."

Ray squeezed Mike's hand, wondering if Mrs Shriver would be as kind and welcoming as her sons. They entered the living room to find Barbara Shriver talking to Rhonda and Abby, Ben's wife. For a seventy-eight-year-old woman, Barbara was incredibly bright-eyed.

"Mom," Mike greeted the woman with a hug and kiss on the cheek. "I swear you get more beautiful every time I see you," he heard Mike whisper in her ear.

"Flattery will get you dinner on Sunday," she said in return.

Mike released his mom and held out his hand to Ray. "I'd like you to meet Ray DeMonico, the love of my life," Mike added, much to Ray's surprise and embarrassment.

Barbara wrapped her thin arms around Ray's shoulders and hugged him. "It's so nice to finally meet you. Michael talks about you every time we speak on the phone."

Ray glanced at Mike. "Good things, I hope."

"The best," she confirmed. Barbara moved to cup Ray's cheeks in her hands. "He said you were handsome, but he didn't tell me you were good-looking enough to be on one of my soap operas."

Ray felt his face flush. "Thank you."

"Can I get you something to drink, Mom?" Mike asked.

"A glass of wine would be nice," she answered without looking at Mike. She took Ray's hand and pulled him towards the dining room. "Come in here and let's get to know each other."

"Yes, ma'am."

Ray sat beside Barbara and wished he was anywhere else. "So, Mike tells me you still teach classes at the community centre."

"Quilting, but only two nights a week. I know I'm too old for it, but I'm afraid if the younger generation doesn't learn, it will soon be a forgotten art form."

Ray had never thought of quilts as art, but he could understand the comparison.

Barbara leaned closer to Ray. "Mike hasn't come out and told me, but I have a feeling he's going to move away from us, is that right?"

Trapped, Ray wasn't sure how to answer. Lying, however, wasn't an option. "He's made the offer."

"Why don't you seem thrilled?" she asked.

"Because what's waiting for him in Kansas City is nothing compared to what he has here," Ray admitted.

"You don't love him?"

"Of course I love him, that's why this is so hard."

Barbara patted Ray's hand where it rested on the table. "Michael's a big boy, perfectly capable of making his own decisions. I'm sure he wouldn't have offered if he didn't feel it was important enough to give up his life here."

Mike came into the room with two glasses of red wine and a fresh beer. "Is she telling stories on me?"

Ray accepted his wine. "We were talking about quilting."

When Mike started in on the subject of his mom's passion for quilting, Ray sat back and listened. It was obvious how much Mike adored his mom, and Ray couldn't help but wonder how much longer Barbara would be around. It was one more thing that had Ray questioning Mike's decision to move.

Always the businessman, Ray began putting their situation into perspective. As he half-listened to Mike and his mother's conversation, he began to get a clearer picture of what exactly was on the line. The biggest question he needed to answer for himself was, was it worth sacrificing their relationship for?

* * * *

Ray woke the next morning feeling guilty. He'd overheard Ben tell Mike that Sidney still hadn't returned to work. Although he knew Mike had been getting updates on Sidney's partner's condition, Mike had gone out of his way not to mention Sidney's name in front of him. Being forced to choose between his concern for a dear friend and a jealous boyfriend was a hell of a fix for Mike to be in. "You should go see Sidney and Nash today," he announced over breakfast.

Mike set down his coffee. "Excuse me?"

Ray had slept very little since his epiphany at Steven's house, and one conclusion he'd come to was the importance of making peace with Mike's relationship with Sidney. He took a deep breath, knowing the next few minutes could change his life forever. "I know you care about your friends, and if I'm going to relocate here, it's important that I find a way to deal with your feelings for Sidney."

"Wait." Mike began to wave his hands as if to ward off Ray's words. "What? There are so many things wrong with what you just said that I don't know where to begin. First and foremost, I've worked out whatever feelings I used to have for Sidney. I've realised since being with you, that it wasn't Sidney I was so in love with as much as the way Sidney loved Nash." Mike held his hands out, silently asking for Ray's in return.

Ray touched his palms against Mike's.

"Sidney is, and always will be, special to me, but you're the one I'm in love with. You're the one who's opened my eyes to feelings I've never known before but have always desired. And there's no way in hell I'm going to let you give up that club for me."

"Why not? It's a building. You're willing to give up a home you love, a family you adore and a business you've built with your brothers. It only makes sense if you weigh the pros and cons. The athletic club gave me a purpose, something to focus on besides my unfulfilling relationship. I don't need that anymore."

Mike stood and leaned over the table to kiss Ray. "What if you start to resent me for giving up everything you've worked so hard for?"

"Won't happen. I'll be getting so much more than I'm leaving that it's not really even a hard decision once I stopped long enough to really think about it. I don't plan on selling my share of the business, but if I can find someone qualified to take over as general manager, I can still be involved to some degree."

"I have a feeling Brent won't like it." Mike grinned. "But I do." He lifted Ray's hands to his mouth and kissed them both. "You won't regret it, I swear. I'll spend the rest of my life thanking you for this."

"For someone who was all set to move to Kansas City, you seem awfully happy about staying here."

Mike shrugged. "I would've moved anywhere or done anything to be with you, but I'll admit, I love it here. And I swear you will, too."

"You won't make me shovel snow, will you?"

"Never. The driveway and walks are heated. Why do you think I talked you into putting in that system at the club?"

Ray was still nervous about giving up one dream in Kansas City to follow another in Chicago, but as long as Brent agreed to Ray's role as limited partner, he wouldn't have to give up anything at all. Regardless, Ray knew where his future lay and it was just north of the windy city.

SOUL
RESTORATION

Dedication

I have received several emails from a very polite gentleman asking when the next story of this series would be written. Well, here it is. I hope you enjoy it. I've tried numerous times to email you back, but all my emails are returned as undeliverable. Sorry, but I hope this makes up for it.

Chapter One

"Hey, Pete, John wants you to head over to the Wilson job after you finish here," Brent barked, shoving his cell phone in his pocket.

"Sure thing," Pete Braxton answered. He opened the last bag of coco shell mulch and sprinkled it around the freshly planted fountain grass. It was almost five, which meant he'd get overtime for making the trip across town. *Cool.* He could use some extra cash. With a leaking water heater and his truck payment overdue by a week, anything beyond his normal six hundred a week was gravy.

After quickly cleaning up his supplies, Pete climbed behind the wheel of the company truck and took a left out of the driveway. When the local news came on the radio, he reached for the knob to change the station but stopped when he heard his brother's name.

"In overnight news, Shawnee Mission Parkway was the scene of a deadly head-on collision. Both drivers, Braxton Investments owner and CEO, David Braxton, and Wayne Potts of Lenexa were killed instantly."

Pete slammed his fist against the knob, effectively breaking the radio and splitting his knuckle open. "Fuck." He shook his hand while looking for the nearest place to pull over. Despite their estrangement, he'd always hoped there'd be time to make up, to become brothers once again. That wouldn't happen now. It was over. He was well and truly on his own. Coming to a stop in a grocery store parking lot, Pete searched through the glove box and finally came up with a couple of drive-thru paper napkins.

What now? What was a brother who wasn't wanted supposed to do? Pete felt lost, like he was adrift without a boat. Which didn't make any sense since he'd been on his own for almost ten years, but having a brother who didn't want him was different than having no brother at all.

How can I be mad at a dead man?

Pete's phone rang, startling him. He glanced at the caller ID before answering. "Hey."

"Where're you at?" John, Pete's boss and the owner of the landscaping company, asked. "Brent called and told me you left, but that was over thirty minutes ago."

Pete looked at the clock on the dashboard. *Jesus Christ, how long have I been sitting here?* "Sorry, I just heard some bad news," he mumbled.

John cleared his throat. "So you heard. Sorry, man, that's why I wanted to see you. The police called looking for you, but I didn't want them to get to you first. News like that…"

"Yeah." Pete swallowed. "So, am I supposed to call the police or something?"

John paused. "David's body's already been identified by his secretary. I think the police were just looking to inform the next of kin of his death."

Pete nodded to himself. It felt weird to hear himself referred to as David's next of kin. Sure, technically, he was, but David had readily gone along with his father's wish to have Pete out of the family and their lives. "Okay."

"They told me if I saw you to have you call David's lawyer. I've got a number right here."

"Miller, Cambridge and Stone, right?" Pete recited the name of the law firm the Braxton family had used for years.

"No, actually, it's a man named Matthew Field. He's got an office out in the 'burbs somewhere," John corrected.

Matthew Field. "I'll give him a call."

"You need a few days off?" John asked.

"Not sure yet. I'll give you a call as soon as I figure it out." Pete knew he hadn't processed the news of his brother's death because he still wasn't sure how he was supposed to feel about it. Was it callous to hate someone who'd just died? "Thanks, John."

"Call if you need anything," John said before hanging up.

Pete took several calming breaths before heading home, back to the one bedroom house he shared with Cheddar, a huge, long-haired orange cat.

The minute Pete stepped into the house the cat was there, waiting for him. Cheddar's favourite means of getting attention was to headbutt Pete's calf until he got what he wanted. "In a minute," he said, ripping the napkin from his hand. The cut to his knuckle had dried, but he'd need to get it cleaned up eventually.

He opened the old console stereo he'd bought at a second-hand store down the street and withdrew the yellow-paged phone directory. While searching the attorney section, he was continually assaulted by

Cheddar. Pete ripped out the page with Field's phone number. "Okay, dinner, got it," he told the cat.

Cheddar let out a mew that sounded more like a cuss word.

Pete rolled his eyes and stuck the page to the fridge with a take-out menu magnet. "Technically, it's not even time for you to eat, so don't get all snippy with me."

Nonplussed by the admonishment, Cheddar sauntered over to his food bowl and plopped onto his side. He stared up at Pete and yawned, evidently trying his damnedest to exert his dominance over the situation.

"Fine, for that, I'm not even going to wash my hands before I get your dinner." Pete retrieved a can of cat food out of the cabinet and used the easy-open pull. His odd relationship with Cheddar had been his lifeline for years.

Pete filled the chipped pottery food bowl and rubbed his companion behind the ears. "Okay, I'm not mad anymore."

Cheddar didn't bother looking up from his dinner, obviously unconcerned with Pete's mood when he had a bowl of flaked tuna and cheese in front of him. Cats definitely weren't meant for people who suffered from low self-esteem. Pete loved Cheddar, but other than the occasional purr and rub against him, his beloved pet rarely gave more than a sympathetic ear. Well, two, but most of the time Pete felt Cheddar was only half listening to him.

"So, my brother died last night," Pete informed his furry friend while getting a beer out of the fridge. "I haven't seen David in...hell, nearly eight years." He glanced down at Cheddar. "It was before you came along, so no need for you to feel jealous. I saw him at a restaurant on The Plaza. I looked up from my twenty-first birthday celebrative steak dinner to find him standing five feet away from my table. At first I thought he was glad to see me, but just as quickly, he shut down and turned away."

Pete upended his can and walked to the living room, leaving Cheddar to finish his dinner in peace. The recliner he'd picked up on Craig's List fit his ass perfectly. It was an ugly gold colour and beyond its prime, but it was his. He grabbed the remote and turned on the local news. As a landscaper, the most important segment had always been the weather, but he barely heard the teaser the meteorologist gave at the top of the hour about the chance of precipitation coming up in the extended forecast.

When a publicity picture of his brother came on screen, Pete sat transfixed. *Older.* David looked so much older, like the life—the vitality—had been sucked right out of him. Is that what running a multi-million dollar investment firm did to a person, or could it have something to do with trying to live up to his father's demands? Not that dear old Dad was demanding much since his death three years earlier.

Pete had also heard that tidbit on the news. Although he hadn't gone to the funeral, he'd hoped that David would reach out to him. Of course, that hadn't happened. It seemed their father hadn't been the barrier between them after all.

Instead, Pete had briefly mourned the loss of his father before moving on with his life. His millionaire father had thrust him into the world of the working poor only a month after Pete's mother had died. As a college freshman who had never before held a job, it hadn't been easy for Pete to take the five thousand dollar check he'd been given by his dad's attorney and start a new life, but he'd done it.

Looking around the living room, Pete studied the cracks in the ceiling and the walls that could use a fresh coat of paint. It was nothing like the 1920's mansion he'd grown up in, but he'd bought it with his own money after saving for over five years. He'd always referred to his six hundred and thirty square foot bungalow as the house that desperation built.

Cheddar jumped onto his lap and began making an imaginary nest for himself. Pete ran his hand down Cheddar's back, soothing his huge companion into settling down. The day he'd closed on the house, a matted ball of orange fur had been waiting for him under the front porch. It had taken Pete a good two hours to discern where the mew was coming from, but using a flashlight, he'd finally found the kitten and had lured him out with the only thing he'd had on hand, a slice of cheese. It hadn't been cheddar cheese, but cheese was a stupid name for a cat. Of course, most people thought Cheddar was just as dumb, but the moment he'd held that kitten in his arms, the name had come to him and had stuck.

"And here you are." Pete grinned. If anyone had told him he'd turn into a cat lover, he'd have punched them, but Cheddar totally had control of the largely unused organ that had been shredded by people who were supposed to love him. "You love me, don't you?"

Cheddar didn't bother to open his eyes at the question. Despite the cat's current indifference, Pete knew Cheddar loved him. Several months earlier, Pete had come down with a wicked case of the flu, and for nearly a week, Cheddar hadn't left his side, even forgoing his daily prowl of the yard.

The phone rang, prompting Pete to mute the television. It didn't matter. He wasn't watching it anyway. "Hello?"

"Peter Braxton?" a deep voice asked.

"Yeah."

"This is Matthew Field."

"Yes, John told me to call you," Pete answered. "I found your number in the book, but I figured I'd just call you tomorrow."

"Yes, and under normal circumstances, I would've waited at least a week to contact you, but unfortunately, David left you everything."

"I'm sorry, Mr Field, but that doesn't make any sense. David hated me." Saying it aloud stung, but Pete had to level with the man.

"Call me Matthew. And David was very specific when he came in and drafted his will. I know this may be hard for you to understand, but I think he was trying to right some wrongs."

"Maybe he shoulda done it while he was still alive. I could've gone anywhere after they kicked me out, but I chose to make my life here in case David changed his mind. Now you call and tell me he wanted to make things right? Sorry, I don't buy it." Pete took a deep breath. It wasn't Matthew's fault, and he needed to remember that.

"I've been David's friend for years, and even I don't know why he cut you out like he did. He refused to talk about it, but he does have a sealed envelope here with your name on it. If nothing else, maybe that'll explain something." Matthew cleared his throat. "There's something else. David had a dog."

"A dog? You are talking about David James Braxton, right?" Pete couldn't imagine the David he'd grown up with owning and caring for a pet, especially a stinky dog.

"Hard to believe, but he fell in love with an English Bulldog at our fraternity house at school and decided to get one after your father's death."

"And you want me to head over to his house to take care of the dog," Pete surmised. The last thing Pete wanted to do was get out again, but he couldn't stand the thought of the dog crapping all over his mom's house. "What's the dog's name?"

"Julie. She's white with a few small patches of light brown."

Pete stared down at Cheddar. He couldn't imagine bringing a dog into Cheddar's territory. "You wanna dog?" he asked Matthew.

"Sorry. My kids are allergic. Besides, according to David's will, the dog has to stay with the house."

"I've got a house," Pete said. "The entire thing may be able to fit into the foyer of the Braxton Mansion, but it's mine."

"And so is the Braxton Mansion," Matthew reminded Pete. "I know David's death's come as a shock, but there're a lot of people who depend on your family to make a living. With your father and David both gone there are certain decisions you'll have to make."

"I'm not an investment banker," Pete growled, losing his temper. "Never had the training, thanks to my father."

When Matthew didn't reply, Pete knew he'd sounded like a spoilt child. "Sorry. You didn't deserve that," he apologised.

"It's okay. It's been a rough day for both of us. If you'll meet me at the house, I can give you the keys and codes."

"Yeah, sure. Give me twenty minutes." Pete hung up. "Sorry, Cheddar, but I have to go out." He still wasn't sure what he was going to do with David's dog, but he had no plans of staying the night.

"I'll be back before you miss me," he said, grabbing his keys and ball cap on the way out of the door.

* * * *

Pete beat Matthew to the house, so he pulled as close to the eight-foot iron gates as he dared, hoping the bed of his truck was far enough out of the street. A sedan pulled in beside him and the ornate gates swung inward.

A handsome man in his mid-thirties gestured for Pete to lead the way up the long drive. Pete nodded in acknowledgement before putting the truck in gear and taking off. Back in his younger days, he'd have seen how fast he could make it from Ward Parkway to the garage bay reserved for him, but those days were behind him, and he was driving a company truck.

Although the expansive grounds were still lit up like a runway, the flowerbeds that used to line the driveway, surround each tree and curve gracefully around the front of the house were gone, replaced with heavily manicured bushes that looked like a damn bunch of poodles wandering the lawn. "Fuck."

Pete got out of the truck and waited for Matthew. "What the hell happened to Mom's flowerbeds?"

Dressed in jeans, a plaid shirt and a navy sports jacket, Matthew adjusted his baseball cap and shook his head. "Just wait'll you see what David did to the inside." He pulled a set of keys out of his pocket and climbed the steps. "He went through something about six months after your dad died." He opened the door and immediately punched a series of numbers into the keypad just inside.

Pete's breath caught in his chest as he stepped into the foyer. The sweeping mahogany staircase that had rivalled the one from *Gone with the Wind* was gone, replaced with a cheap generic one that didn't even fit the space. The aged, but glossy floorboards had been ripped up as well as all the ornate moulding.

"And that's not all." Matthew made a left and continued into the living room. "David ripped it all out, every bit of it."

Pete wiped the sweat from his forehead as his stomach turned over. "Holy fuck." The huge room was a shell, nothing more. The woodwork had been stripped, the plaster walls torn out, leaving only studs and insulation behind. He felt violated. Memories of his mom had comforted him after what his father had done, but as he studied the destruction, the thoughts that had sustained him evaporated. "Why?"

"I don't know. He started seeing a counsellor not long after he did this, till just last week, as far as I know." Matthew rubbed the back of his neck.

"It looks like he hated this house, but if that was the case, why not just sell the damn thing and move?" Pete ducked into the dining room and found the same state of disarray.

"Come on, I need to show you something." Matthew headed out of the living room before climbing the stairs. "David didn't spend time down here. As far as I know, he spent it all in his bedroom suite. That's where we'll find Julie."

Pete followed Matthew. "How close were the two of you?"

"He's…" Matthew shook his head. "He *was* my children's godfather. We were roommates for five years at KU. We were close." He laughed. "Well, as close as David was with anyone, I suppose."

It didn't make sense to Pete. David had been out of college before Pete had graduated high school. "If you and David were so close, why haven't I met you?"

With his hand on the doorknob to David's room, Matthew shook his head. "I don't know. David wouldn't let me come over when we were off for breaks and stuff. I always assumed your parents were alcoholics or something, but I met your dad on a few occasions and he barely drank."

"My father drank socially, but Mom didn't at all. Actually, now that you say that, I don't remember any of David's friends coming around when I was growing up." Why hadn't that stuck out in his mind before? David had always been popular. Hell, Pete had walked in his brother's shadow at the expensive Catholic school he'd been forced to attend, so why hadn't his friends come around the house?

"This'll look familiar," Matthew said, opening the door.

Compared to the destruction of the downstairs, David's room seemed to pull him inside, welcoming him with open arms. "Not much has changed in here." He grinned at the framed art on the walls. "Except the posters are a lot more expensive."

A lazy bark came from the foot of the king-sized bed. It seemed Julie was aware of the intruders, but wasn't concerned enough to climb down the mini-staircase to investigate them. If the dog's lack of gumption held true, Julie and Cheddar should be able to tolerate each other, although there was no way in hell Pete was sharing a bed with the bulldog.

Pete walked towards the bed, but stopped when something caught his attention. Changing direction, he plucked a leather-bound photo album off the desk. "This was Mom's." He remembered because he used to spend hours looking at it. "I'm gonna take this."

"You're leaving?" Matthew asked.

Pete glanced at the bed. "Don't worry. The dog goes with me. It'll take me a few days to deal with this shit, and I have no intentions of trying to get my head on straight while living in this house."

* * * *

After an incredibly loud and rocky twelve hours, Cheddar and Julie managed to reach an amicable truce. Julie found a corner of the couch that she was allowed to lie in, and Cheddar maintained control of the rest of the house. It wasn't the perfect situation, but it would work for the time being.

Pete sat in his favourite chair, flipping through the photo album. He'd stared at each picture so long he could probably draw the damn things in detail. Stopping on his favourite, Pete traced the outline of his mom's image. It had been taken the Christmas before he'd graduated high school. God, he couldn't believe how small she was. At five-foot-eleven, Pete was average, but in the picture, his mom barely came to his shoulder. *Weird.* He'd remembered her as being so much bigger. The picture of the carved fireplace mantle behind her was one of the best he'd found.

It was hard to explain, but he needed that fireplace to still be there. He needed to know that something of his childhood still remained intact. Decision made, Pete set the album on the table before picking up his phone.

"How much money are we talking about?" Pete asked.

"Peter?" Matthew sounded like he'd just got out of bed.

"Yeah, sorry to call so early. I haven't been to bed yet, so I guess I lost track of time."

"Hang on." Matthew covered the phone and said something to someone in the room. "Just so you know, I've got a wonderful wife, but I also have three kids who run her ragged every day."

"So, in other words, don't call this early and wake her up," Pete surmised.

"Bingo." Matthew yawned. "So, what was your question again?"

"Do I have enough money to restore the house?" Pete still didn't plan to ever move into his childhood home, but he'd learnt to live without money, so it might as well go to something he believed in.

"You have enough money to buy ten just like it. More, depending on what you want to do with the business."

"Good, because I'm gonna have to find the best craftsman out there and that sure as hell isn't going to come cheap."

"Why, Pete? I don't know everything, but I know your father kicked you out after your mother's death. How can that man's house mean so much to you?" Matthew questioned.

Pete didn't expect Matthew to understand. Shit, he didn't expect anyone to understand. "I just need that part of my life put back together."

"Okay, I'll get moving on it as soon as I get to the office. David's will's airtight, so we shouldn't have any problem getting you the money."

"Cool, then I'm going to call a friend of mine and see if he can hook me up." Pete glanced at the album. "What about funeral arrangements?"

"Taken care of. I'll know for sure today, but I think this Saturday will be the services. Once I hear from them, I'll contact the newspaper."

Pete's eyes filled with tears, but he quickly blinked the moisture away. *No.* He'd already mourned the loss of his brother years earlier, and he had no more tears for a man who could so easily turn his back on him. "I appreciate you taking care of that."

"It's the least I can do. I told you, David was a good friend," Matthew said, his voice thick with emotion.

"Yeah. He was lucky to have you." Other than John and a few guys he worked with, Pete didn't have many friends. "I'll be here most of the day. Give me a call when you have a date and time for the service."

"Will do."

Pete hung up and scrolled through his contact list until he came up with Mike Shriver's number. He'd only known Mike for about six months, but the co-owner of Brookside Athletic Club had done one hell of a job on the new building, making new construction look like it had been in the Brookside neighbourhood for years.

"Hello?"

"Hey, Mike, it's Pete. Sorry to call so early."

"No problem. Ray and I just got back from our morning run. I heard the news about your brother. Sorry, man."

"Yeah, it came as quite a shock, but even worse, he somehow managed to tear up the house we grew up in. I need the name of someone you trust who can reconstruct all the woodwork that was destroyed."

"Depends on how much you want to spend. The best is William Oliver. He takes his time to do the job right, but he's expensive."

"Money's not a problem if I can get what I want. You got a number for him?" Pete asked.

"No, but his grandson put a website together for him." Mike rattled off the web address. "By the way, Ray wants to know when we can plant the elephant ear bulbs we bought."

"I get this guy of yours to restore my house, and I'll come over and plant them for you," Pete offered. He'd drawn up the new landscape plans for Ray and Mike, the least he could do was help them.

"I'll hold you to that."

"Talk to you later." Pete hung up and glanced at Julie. "You have internet at your place?"

Chapter Two

"Hey, Pops, an email came through from a man in Kansas City, some friend of Mike Shriver. He has a huge job he wants us for." Dylan Oliver handed his phone over to his grandpop.

The old man waved the phone away. "You know I can't stand those things. They give you cancer."

"You can't get cancer from looking at the email," Dylan argued. He should save his breath. There was no way Pops would believe him anyway. "You think you're up to a trip to Kansas City?"

"No." Pops set down his coffee. "I told you after you took this one, my hands can't take another job. It's time you went out on your own."

Dylan had apprenticed for his grandfather since he had been old enough to hold a chisel, but that didn't mean he wanted to strike out on his own. "I need you there."

"No you don't. You're better than I ever was." Pops got to his feet and rested a hand on top of Dylan's head. "We both know it's time for you to be the man you're meant to be."

Dylan stared up into his grandpop's clouded blue eyes. He'd never told anyone about the men he'd slept with, but there was something in Pop's eyes that told him he knew. "Will you still be here for me when I get back?"

"Where else would I be?" Pops squeezed Dylan's shoulder before carrying his empty cup to the sink. "Call that man back, and tell him you'll take the job."

Dylan wrote the phone number on a piece of scrap paper and took another look at the pictures attached to the email. The house would take every ounce of skill he possessed, but he'd learnt first-hand from the master.

Kansas City. It would be the first time he'd travelled alone for a job. Dylan wondered what it would be like to openly engage in a lifestyle he'd fought so hard to hide from his grandmom and grandpop. *Freeing*, he surmised.

* * * *

Pete pulled Julie to a stop as he answered his phone, "Hello?"

"Peter Braxton?" a deep voice asked.

"Pete," he corrected.

"Okay, Pete, this is Dylan Oliver. You sent an email to my grandfather, William, about a job?"

"Yes. I got his name from a mutual friend, Mike Shriver. He and his partner own a new athletic club here in town. Mike told me your grandfather is the best. Is he interested?" At Julie's insistence, Pete started walking the lawn again.

"Well, that's the thing. Pops isn't well enough to travel, but I've got the time."

Shit. Pete wanted to scream, but Dylan didn't deserve his frustration. "Sorry, but I need the best. This project means a lot to me, everything actually."

"I've studied from the best for over twenty years. I've got photos of my work if that helps. You can call Mike if you don't believe me." Dylan sighed. "Please, at least consider it. I need to get away from home for a while."

It wasn't hard to hear the desperation in Dylan's voice. Yeah, he'd been there. "Can you send the pics to my phone?"

"Yeah, definitely. As soon as we hang up, I'll get them over to you," Dylan said.

"Okay, send them, and I'll call back." Pete hung up and waited.

By the time Julie had taken care of business, Pete was scrolling through pictures. "Damn, if he really did this work, he's good." He didn't hesitate to call Dylan back.

"Did you get 'em?" Dylan asked, answering the phone.

"Yep. When can you start?" Pete asked.

"As soon as I can get there and find a place to stay. Unfortunately, we also need to discuss money. It's a huge job, bigger than any I've ever done, so it'll take some time."

"I figured that. As far as a place to live, you can stay in the house if you want. I've got my own place, so you don't need to worry about me getting in your way. You'll be paid whatever it takes to get the job done right."

"It could be upwards of a hundred G's, you know that, right?"

"I'll double it if it'll get the work done faster." The sooner the house was put back the way it was, the sooner Pete could move on with his life. "My brother's funeral's tomorrow. If you could get here the day after, I'd appreciate it."

"I'll be there. Just send me the address, and I'll meet you at the house," Dylan said.

"That's okay, I can pick you up at the airport if you let me know your flight time," Pete offered. He wondered if David had still enjoyed his cars as much as he used to.

"Thanks, but I'll drive down. No way all my tools will fit into a couple of bags. Besides, they hold sentimental value, and I can't take the chance of them getting lost. I'll leave tonight. I shouldn't have a problem getting to Kansas City by Sunday."

"Great." Pete rattled off the address. "Got it?"

"Yeah, I'll find it. See you then, and thanks again for the opportunity," Dylan said.

"You might not feel the same way once you've seen the state of this house." Pete liked the sound of Dylan's voice — deep, masculine.

"I love a challenge." Dylan chuckled. "See you Sunday."

Pete stuck the phone in his pocket. He wondered if it was possible to be attracted to a man just from the sound of his voice?

* * * *

Dressed in the nicest clothes he had, Pete stood next to John at the graveside service. It was the first time he'd ever seen John in a suit. The perfectly tailored pin-stripe looked off for some reason. Maybe because he was used to seeing the big bald man in T-shirts with the sleeves cut off to accommodate the size of his biceps.

"You doing okay?" John asked, lowering his sunglasses to look Pete in the eyes.

Pete nodded. He couldn't believe the number of people in attendance. Moreover, he only recognised a few of them.

Pete's Uncle Stuart kept giving him the hairy eyeball, which didn't surprise Pete in the least. No doubt his dad's family felt they deserved a chunk of the Braxton pie, but unless Pete gave it to them, it wasn't happening.

He smiled at his uncle. *Not gonna happen, asshole.*

Uncle Stuart had been one of the first people Pete had reached out to when his father had cut him off. Unfortunately, his uncle had turned him away without batting an eyelash, afraid of going against the man with all the money.

Fucker.

"You know that man?" John asked.

"Yep, and he'll be kissing my ass as soon as this service is over." Pete glanced at John. "I guarantee it."

"Want me to run interference?"

"No, actually, I'm looking forward to it." When prompted by David's priest, Pete stepped forward and pulled a blood-red rose out of the floral spray. "Thank you," he told the priest.

A sobbing woman stepped towards the casket and also took a flower. Pete didn't know her, but by the anguish she displayed, David had been close to her. He moved to stand next to Matthew and his wife. "Is that David's girlfriend?"

Matthew nodded. "Jodi. Her and David had had an on again, off again thing for the past four years. Nice lady."

Jodi was an attractive woman, but not the typical blonde bombshell David had dated in high school. "So why the on again, off again?"

"She wanted a commitment from him. When she didn't get one, she'd leave, he'd play the field for a couple of months, realise there was nothing better out there and beg her for another chance." Matthew shrugged. "Cycle. The damn shame is that I believe he really did love her. David just wasn't able to commit for some reason."

Poor woman. Pete knew what it felt like to be rebuffed by David. "I'd like to talk to her."

After ending the service with a prayer, the priest approached Pete. "Take comfort in knowing that David didn't suffer, and he's with your mother and father."

"Thank you." Pete shook the priest's hand.

When the priest turned to offer more words of wisdom to the next person in line, Pete sought out Matthew.

"Jodi, this is Pete, David's younger brother," Matthew introduced.

Jodi looked surprised. "It's nice to meet you."

"You didn't know about me, did you?" Pete could tell by Jodi's expression that his beloved brother had never mentioned him.

Jodi crossed her arms over her chest. "David told me his brother died."

Although he should've known David would explain away his existence in such a pitiful way, actually hearing the words cut deep. "Excuse me."

Without looking back, Pete headed for John's truck. He heard footsteps running up behind him, but didn't stop.

"You need a beer?" John took off the suit jacket and tossed it in the back before getting in.

"Nope. Tequila." Pete climbed in and shut the door. He was holding onto his emotions by a thread and drinking was probably the last thing he needed to do, but drowning his sorrows in a bottle was better than taking a shotgun to the Porsche his brother had in the garage.

"You want some company?" John asked, pulling the truck around the parked hearse.

"Thanks, but I think I'd rather be alone right now. Besides, I still have Uncle Stuart to deal with. You can do me a favour, though."

"Name it," John said.

"Drop me by my brother's house, then go over to my place and make sure the animals have food and water." Pete rolled down the window and leaned his head against the back of the seat.

"You're not gonna do anything stupid are you?"

"Don't plan on it, but I don't have the energy to take care of anything but me right now." Pete turned his head towards his friend. John had hired him for his first job. "Can I ask you something?"

"Sure."

"Why'd you hire me?" Pete asked.

"Huh?"

"You had to know I didn't know the first thing about cutting grass or trimming bushes, so why'd you take a chance on me?" Pete still remembered the crash course John had given him that first day. The patience John had shown in the beginning had earned him a loyal employee for life. "Why me and not some other kid?"

"I saw real, bottom of the barrel desperation in you that day. Once you see that look in a man, you never forget and you don't turn your back on him."

Despite the ache in his heart, Pete grinned. "Is that some of that Dr Phil shit?"

"Fucker," John mumbled. "You need me to stop at the liquor store?"

"Naw, David's got a well-stocked bar." Pete turned sideways in the seat. "I'd like to take a next week off if it's okay. I've got a guy driving in tomorrow from Portland, Maine, to restore the house. I also need to figure out what the hell to do with Braxton Investments."

"You thinking of giving up the landscaping business for a suit and tie?" John asked.

"I'd sooner put a gun to my head. No, I just need to figure out if I should sell it or find someone to run the damn thing for me. Matthew said he'd walk me through all that stuff." When they neared the house, Pete pulled the gate remote out of his pocket and hit the button.

"Take all the time you need, but I might need the truck mid-week."

"No problem." Pete stared at the empty flowerbeds on their way up the drive. "Can I buy some flowers wholesale?"

"Of course. You know our suppliers as well as I do, call 'em." John stopped in front of the house. "Call me if you need to talk."

"Will do. Thanks." Pete slapped John on the arm before getting out of the truck.

* * * *

Pete was pouring his third shot of tequila when the front gate buzzer sounded. "Right on time, Uncle Stuart."

Without bothering to talk to the man over the intercom, Pete pressed the button that would open the gates. He looked around at the destruction, and quickly decided not to share David's breakdown with someone who had the power to contest the will.

Pete opened the front door and watched a black sedan pull up the drive. He closed the door behind him in an attempt to let his uncle know he wasn't welcome. Standing on the top step, he crossed his arms and prepared himself for the argument he knew was coming. He'd never thought of himself as a cruel man, but he had just enough anger in him to treat his uncle the way he'd been treated when he'd reached out for help.

"Petey," Stuart greeted, getting out of the car.

"What do you want?" Pete asked.

"Is that any way to greet your only uncle? I didn't get a chance to talk to you at the cemetery, so I thought I'd come by and see how you're holding up."

"Bullshit. You came by to see if David left a piece of the pie for you, and the answer is no." Pete tilted his head to the side. "That is why you really came, right?"

"We're talking millions of dollars. All I need is half a million to keep me from losing my house. David paid the mortgage and without him... I'll lose everything. Surely you can give me that," Stuart pleaded. "It's what David would've wanted."

"If David wanted you to have something, he would've left it to you. You can barely hold a job. You have no business buying an expensive house in the first place." Pete chuckled, getting more satisfaction out of the situation than he probably should have. "So,

I'll tell you what you told me when I asked for help. Life is hard. It's time you learned to stand on your own two feet."

Stuart's face went red. "You do this, and I'll make sure David's fortune is tied up in the courts until you're a very old man."

So predictable. Pete laughed. "You do that. You've got what, maybe another ten, fifteen years before your liver gives out? If you want to spend every dime you make in the meantime trying to fight something you can't win, go ahead. You see, I've learned to stand on my own two feet. I guess I have you to thank for that. I don't need David's money, but I'll sure as hell do everything in my power to make sure you don't see a dime of it."

Stuart just stood there, his mouth gaping. "You'd do that to family?"

"*They* did it to *me*." Pete turned and walked back into the house, slamming the door behind him.

* * * *

Seated at David's desk, Pete decided to forego the glass and drink straight from the bottle. He'd cleaned out David's drawers, looking for answers, but all he'd found were financial papers, receipt crap and a bundle of season tickets to the Kansas City Royals baseball team.

Pete ran his fingers over the tickets. David didn't even like baseball. Pete did, though, and took in a game whenever he had the spare cash, which wasn't often. He couldn't help but wonder if he'd been at the stadium, sitting in the cheap seats, while David had wined and dined clients in the private suite. He chuckled, imagining the guys from his crew up in one of those fancy suites.

He briefly wondered if Linc would be interested in going to a game. Pete could count on one hand the number of actual boyfriends he'd had over the years, but Lincoln Hays had been the one man he'd thought would last.

Pete reached for the phone. Without giving himself time to chicken out, he called Linc. It had been almost three months since he'd last spoken to his ex, so maybe things had changed.

"Hey."

Pete sat up straighter. "Hey. You have time to talk?"

"Not really. I'm at a dinner party with Brent." Linc's voice softened. "I was sorry to hear about your brother. Are you doing okay?"

Pete closed his eyes, wrapping Linc's concern around him like a warm blanket. It wasn't often that he let his guard down enough to need someone, but with three-quarters of a bottle of tequila in his gut, his defences were almost non-existent. "I'm okay, I guess, but I need to see you."

"I can't, Pete. You know how Brent is. He's staring at me right now, and I can't screw this up with him."

"Why? You know you don't love him." Pete still didn't understand why Linc had left him. Even more, he didn't understand why he only cared to know when he was drunk.

"Goodbye, Pete. Take care of yourself." Linc hung up without giving Pete an answer.

"Fuck!" Pete threw the phone before picking up his bottle. He'd only met Linc's boyfriend, Brent Atwood, on a couple of occasions at the athletic club, and he hadn't been impressed.

When the phone rang again, Pete scrambled to reach it. "Linc?"

"Umm, no, this is Dylan. Did I call at a bad time?"

Pete rubbed his eye with the heel of his hand. "No, it's fine."

"I know it's not a good day for you, but I made great time, and I'm on the outskirts of the city. I can go ahead and get a hotel room if you'd rather, but I thought I'd give you the option. If I can get into the house tonight, I can start first thing in the morning."

Pete looked at the mess he'd made in David's room. He'd originally planned to let Dylan take the room, but as drunk as he was, there was no way he'd be able to get it cleaned up and drive home. The other option was his parents' old bedroom. He'd only taken a quick peek inside on his tour of the house, but it had looked like it was still set up.

"If it's a bad time, don't worry about it," Dylan said, interrupting Pete's foggy thoughts.

"No, I'm sorry. I'm a little drunk, but if that doesn't scare you off, come on over to the address I gave you. I'll probably need to put fresh sheets on the bed, but that's not a problem."

"Hell, as tired as I am, I could sleep on a mattress without sheets, and don't worry about being drunk. I moonlight as a bouncer at one of our local clubs when work's slow."

"So you're going to toss me out of the house if I get loud?" Pete asked.

Dylan chuckled. "No, just meant I'm a pretty patient guy."

Once again Dylan's deep voice had a direct effect on Pete's cock. "I'll go ahead and open the gate," Pete said.

"Great. I really appreciate it. I spent a few hours last night in the back of my pickup, and while I'd do it again if I needed to, a real bed sounds a hell of a lot better."

"No problem. See ya when you get here." Pete hung up the phone and got to his feet. Leaving the bottle behind, he staggered to the bathroom and started removing his clothes. He couldn't do much about the booze he'd drunk, but he could at least try to sober up with a quick shower.

* * * *

Dylan's GPS led him directly to a well-lit mansion surrounded by a tall, black iron fence. Surely, the address had to be wrong. Pete had said it was a big job, but the house in front of him looked more like a hotel.

As promised, the gates were open and the warm glow of landscape lighting beckoned him up the driveway. By the time he'd parked and was out of his truck, the front door was standing open. Dylan held up his hand. "Pete?"

"Yep." Pete gestured to the steps. "I'd come down and greet you, but knowing my luck, I'd fall on my face."

Dylan grinned. "That far gone, are ya?"

"Tequila," Pete said in explanation.

"Nasty shit." Dylan grabbed his suitcase out of the back. "Will the tools be okay out here?"

"Should be. As far as I know, this place has never been robbed." Pete gestured to the added security lights that had come on when Dylan had pulled up. "I'll leave those on if it'll make you feel better."

Dylan retrieved the heavy canvas bag with the most precious of his tools and set it on the driveway. "I'll take this one. The others can stay." He locked the truck and made his way up the brick steps to come face to face with his new employer.

"Nice to finally meet you." Dylan held out his hand. He could tell by the expression on Pete's incredibly handsome face that he'd surprised him. To lighten the mood, he gave Pete his best smile. "Something tells me you didn't expect a six-foot-eight black man to show up on your doorstep."

"You're right. I gotta be honest, you threw me for a second." Pete shook Dylan's hand. "Sorry about that."

"No need to apologise. I get that reaction a lot," Dylan said, trying to put Pete at ease.

"Come in." Pete grabbed Dylan's suitcase before leading the way into the house.

Dylan's first look rocked him. "Damn, it's even worse than the pictures."

Pete nodded. "I've gathered quite a few photos of the way it looked before my brother went psycho on the place, and I've been calling around, and I think a salvage company downtown might have one of the mantels. The owner sent me a picture this morning, but I told him I had David's funeral to attend. He said he'd hold it for me until Monday."

"That would help." Dylan set his bag of tools down. He pointed to the staircase. "I can't imagine why anyone would do that."

"Me neither." Pete set Dylan's suitcase down by the stairs. "Want a beer?"

"Anything but tequila," Dylan answered, following Pete towards the back of the house. He let his gaze stray to Pete's ass. The blue jeans were faded in all the right places and damn, Pete filled them out perfectly.

"Watch your head," Pete said, entering the kitchen.

Dylan put a hand on the top of the doorframe. "Are they like this all through the house?"

"Mostly. Not the grand openings, but the regular doorways are all around the same height." Pete opened the refrigerator. "Mexican or domestic?"

"Better not spoil me with the good stuff until the job's done." Dylan ducked his head forward an inch or so and entered the kitchen. "This looks relatively untouched by your brother's...reconstruction."

"Yeah." Pete handed Dylan a can of Miller. Their eyes met and held for several moments. Pete broke contact first, leaving Dylan to wonder if he wasn't the only one who felt the attraction. Pete cleared his throat. "Whatever he was going through didn't extend to the kitchen or the upstairs." He shrugged and gestured to the table. "I guess I'd better give you a little background information."

Dylan pulled out a kitchen chair across from Pete. As he sipped his beer, he listened to Pete's story, surprised at how parts of the tale mimicked his own life. Although he hadn't been thrown out of the family, his grandpop and grandmom had raised him, instead of his mother and father.

Despite what Pete's father and brother had done to him, each time Pete mentioned David's name his face softened. Dylan finished his beer and looked for a place to toss the empty. "Mind if I have another?"

"Not at all. Get me another while you're at it."

Dylan stood and retrieved two more beers. "I hope you don't take this the wrong way, but it sounds like your brother was weak." He waved the can of beer in a circle. "All this—what he did to the house, was his way of getting back at your father."

"For what he did to me?" Pete asked.

Dylan shook his head. "I shouldn't have said anything. I don't know what was in David's mind."

Pete reached across the table and grabbed Dylan's wrist. "Tell me what you were going to say."

Dylan stared into Pete's light green eyes. God, they were captivating. "I think David was under your dad's thumb for too many years. The destruction in those rooms is a grown-up temper tantrum. He wasn't getting back at your father for what he'd done to you, but what he'd done to David."

Chapter Three

Pete paused, his beer halfway to his lips, the memory of his twenty-first birthday flashing through his mind. He'd taken the expression in David's eyes that night as hatred, but what if it had been guilt? "No. If David had been under my father's thumb, he would've contacted me after Dad died."

"Unless he was afraid you'd reject him," Dylan offered. With a sigh, he sat back in his chair and held up his hands. "I just need to shut up. Talking people through shit is a bad habit I picked up as a bartender." He took the last gulp of his beer as he got to his feet. "If you'll point me in the direction of my room, I think it's best I turn in for the night."

Pete stared at Dylan's hands before working his gaze the rest of the way up Dylan's body. Jesus, the man was huge. No wonder he didn't want to fly—even a first class seat would be a tight fit. His gaze lingered for a moment on the zipper of Dylan's jeans. "I'll show you."

Dylan smiled down at Pete. "Sounds like a plan."

Shit. Dylan had caught him ogling. Pete ran a hand through his hair. Was Dylan getting ready to get his ass beat or was the smile a sign of acceptance? *Interesting.*

Dylan picked up the empties. "You recycle?"

"Not as much as I should," Pete confessed.

"Time you start." Dylan carried the cans to the sink. "You gotta sack?"

Pete pointed to the cabinet under the sink.

"Get me one?" Dylan asked, rinsing the cans.

When Pete didn't react right away, Dylan turned off the water. "I really need that sack."

Fuck. From the expression on Dylan's face, he knew exactly what he was asking for. Pete moved to stand right next to Dylan before kneeling. He opened the left-hand cabinet door in pretence, giving Dylan permission to move back if he was uncomfortable with the position.

Instead of taking a step back, Dylan shifted his body, ever so slightly, towards Pete. "Before I left home, Pops told me it was time to be the man I was meant to be."

"What's that mean?" Pete asked, his face inches from Dylan's fly.

"That I've spent more than half my life pretending to be someone I'm not." Dylan reached down and threaded his fingers through Pete's hair.

"And what kind of someone is that?" Pete broke eye contact and turned his attention to the growing bulge in Dylan's jeans.

"Straight."

Pete closed his eyes as he pressed his forehead against Dylan's crotch. It wouldn't be the first time he'd blown someone he'd just met, but usually he beat a hasty retreat once they'd both been taken care of.

Unfortunately, if he wanted his mom's house put back together, he needed Dylan to stick around…but God, he wanted Dylan's cock in his mouth and ass.

Dylan moved his hand to Pete's shoulder. "No pressure. I'm sorry if I misread…"

"No. You didn't." Pete grabbed Dylan's heavily muscled thighs and held him in place. "I'm still drunk, and I don't always make the best decisions when I drink."

Dylan sighed. "And I don't always make the best decisions when I'm attracted to someone." He pulled Pete to his feet. "Why don't we give it a pass for the night and see how things stand in the morning?"

The moment was slipping through his fingers and Pete hated the thought of going to bed alone. "Did I also mention I lose all inhibitions when I'm drunk?" Without giving Dylan a chance to reply, Pete walked out of the kitchen, praying Dylan would follow.

Dylan scrubbed a hand over his face as Pete left the room. When he'd looked down to see that mop of dark blond hair pressed against his crotch, he'd nearly come in his jeans, but he'd managed to control himself. He glanced at the doorway. The thought of Pete losing his inhibitions threatened his control once again.

"You coming?" Pete called.

Almost. Dylan adjusted his erection as he walked towards the front of the house. He spotted Pete's shirt at the bottom of the staircase and a pair of jeans draped over the top step.

"I'm waiting…"

Fuck. Dylan took the steps two at a time, ripping his T-shirt off in the process. Tomorrow was another day, and even if he'd driven halfway across the damn country for a piece of ass, he knew he'd never regret it.

Dylan stopped at the top of the steps and unlaced his work boots. "Which room?"

"The one with a naked man in it," Pete answered.

Dylan unzipped his jeans and pushed the rest of his clothes down and off. He gave his cock a couple of strokes as he wandered down the hall. There were only two doors open. He headed towards the first, and bingo, a very naked man was sprawled across the bed. "Waiting for me?"

Pete ran his hands down his body to bracket his stiff cock. "We're both waiting for you."

Dylan entered the room, giving the messy surroundings a cursory glance. "This David's room?"

"Does it matter?" Pete asked.

Dylan rested one knee on the mattress. "Are you going to fire me tomorrow?"

"No. Are you going to leave tomorrow?" Pete shot back, spreading his legs farther apart.

Dylan shook his head. "You have no idea how long I've wanted the chance to live openly." He climbed onto the bed. "As Pops said, to be the man I was meant to be. Looks like Kansas City is that place for me."

Pete rolled to his side and captured the head of Dylan's cock in his mouth. He gave the knob a good suck before pulling back. "And now is the time."

Dylan pulled away momentarily so he could sit with his back to the headboard, then quickly spread his legs and welcomed Pete between them.

Pete crawled up the mattress, putting his face inches from Dylan's cock. He used the tip of his tongue to tickle the crown of Dylan's cock as he stared up at him. "Here's the thing about me and sex," he began, catching a drop of pre-cum on his tongue. "I can go long spells without it, but once I get it, I can't seem to get enough."

My kind of guy. Dylan reached down and traced Pete's lips with the head of his cock. "So you're saying that if we fuck, we'll have to do it again?"

Pete nodded. "And often."

"Sign me up." Dylan groaned as Pete started to suck him. He buried his fingers in Pete's hair and guided him to a rhythm that he liked. "Tell me you've found condoms in this room?"

Pete took Dylan's length as far down his throat as he could – stopping only when he gagged. He sat up and grinned. "Drawer. Lube's in the bathroom." He shrugged. "I took a shower before you got here." He jumped off the bed and practically ran to the bathroom.

Pete's muscular upper body impressed Dylan almost as much as his tight bubble butt. Dylan licked his lips. "You work out?"

Pete disappeared into the bathroom, but was back a second later. "Yeah, but I haven't been at it long. I did some landscape drawings for Mike and his partner, Ray, and in exchange, they gave me a membership to their club." He tossed Dylan the bottle of lube. "Why? Can you tell?"

Dylan ran his hand down Pete's washboard abs. "Definitely."

Pete countered by cupping Dylan's incredibly pronounced pectoral muscles. "I don't even need to ask you, do I?"

Dylan chuckled and pulled Pete onto his lap. He stared at Pete's lips and wondered if the man kissed as well as he sucked. "Actually, not much, but holding a hammer and chisel all day is good for the body."

Pete got to his knees and wrapped his arms around Dylan's neck. "It's definitely good for the body."

Dylan held the back of Pete's head and pulled him in for a kiss. He played his tongue across Pete's before delving deeper.

Pete began to grind his erection against Dylan's stomach. "Shit," he said, breaking the kiss. He reached for the lube Dylan had set on the bed. "Touch me."

Dylan held out his hand while Pete poured a good amount of lube onto his fingers. He'd been right. Pete absolutely knew how to kiss. *Fuck.* He'd hit the jackpot. "Hold yourself open for me," he instructed.

Pete reached behind him and separated the cheeks of his ass.

"Perfect." Dylan used his middle finger to circle the puckered skin of Pete's hole. "How long's it been?"

"My ex broke up with me a little over three months ago," Pete replied.

Dylan eased his middle finger into Pete's hole as he tried to figure out what had gone wrong between Pete and his ex. "What's the name of this ex of yours?"

"Lincoln." Pete moved up and down, riding Dylan's finger. "He found someone else. A slut from the club, with money."

Dylan felt a twinge of jealousy. "He's an idiot."

"Yeah, he is. Brent's money comes from his father. I should know better than anyone how quickly it can be taken away. I tried to tell Linc that, but he said he'd ride the gravy train for as long as he could." Pete leant forward and sucked Dylan's lower lip. "No more talk of my ex."

"Agreed." *For now.* Dylan worked two fingers into Pete's hole. "Can you reach the rubber on the table?"

Pete stretched out and snagged the foil packet. "Want me to put it on you?"

"Yeah, unless you want me to pull out of your ass." Dylan could tell by the way Pete's muscles tightened around his fingers, that wasn't what he wanted.

"Hell no, but you're gonna have to work with me on this." Pete ripped open the condom package as he slid off Dylan's lap. "One more taste." He bent over and licked the pre-cum that had dripped down the side of Dylan's cock before sucking the head into his mouth. "Mmm." He sat back and sheathed Dylan's erection. "Love your taste."

Dylan withdrew his fingers and guided Pete back onto his lap. "Remind me to return the favour. I bet you're as sweet as honey."

Pete laughed as he lowered himself. "Now you're sounding like a player."

Dylan grabbed Pete's ass and spread his cheeks. "I thought I made my level of experience pretty clear earlier." He stared into Pete's eyes as he breached the outer ring of muscles. "To be honest, this is the first time I've fucked in a bed."

Pete swivelled his hips until he was fully seated on Dylan's cock, gasping at the stretch and burn. With his mouth gaping open, he shook his head. "Fuck, you're big."

"Yeah, but you'll appreciate it once you get used to it." Dylan closed his eyes and rested his head back. It was so much better than fucking someone over a sink in a bar bathroom or worse over a toilet in a public bathroom.

"I've never been known for my patience," Pete said as he started to move. He braced his hands on Dylan's shoulders and eased up before lowering himself again.

Dylan was more than impressed at Pete's tenacity. "Easy," he warned.

"No," Pete moaned. "It's good, so good."

When Dylan thought Pete could handle it, he wrapped his arms around Pete's waist and rolled them, putting Pete under him. "You ready?"

"Fuck me." Pete pulled Dylan's head down for a kiss.

Despite the fatigue of hours on the road, Dylan's body responded to the new position with renewed energy. He continued kissing Pete as he fucked the hell out of him.

After a few minutes of hard thrusts, Pete broke the kiss. He wrapped his legs higher around Dylan's waist and crossed them at the ankles. "My ass is gonna be ruined for any other cock."

"Good," Dylan grunted, feeling his climax approaching. "I'm close," he warned.

"Uh huh, me, too," Pete gasped.

With one last burst of energy, Dylan slammed in and out of Pete's ass with breakneck speed, hoping to set Pete off. Within moments, Pete cried out, quickly followed by Dylan. It was the first time he'd ever come at the same time as a partner, made even more special because Pete wasn't a nameless guy. Although they'd only just met, their connection went beyond physical, at least as far as he was concerned.

With his cock still buried inside Pete, Dylan collapsed. "Fuck," he groaned. Between the hours on the road and the workout in bed, Dylan was wiped.

"That completely sobered me up," Pete said once he'd caught his breath.

Dylan pulled out and removed the condom. "Now that you're sober, do you have any regrets?"

"Only one."

Dylan leaned up on his elbow. "What's that?"

"That I'm too tired right now to do it again," Pete mumbled, reaching over the side of the bed to grab the blanket.

As exhausted as Dylan was, he forced himself to get out of bed. He did a quick wash up after disposing of the condom then returned to the bedroom. "Mind if I crash in here?"

He was met by a soft snore. Dylan grinned and climbed back into bed. He straightened the covers and after a few minutes, decided to indulge in a little spooning. It was new for him, something he'd always longed to do. *Nice.* He sighed. *No, better than nice. Fantastic.*

* * * *

Pete was up and out of the house early the following morning. His night with Dylan had changed things. The original plan had been to hand the Braxton Mansion over to Dylan for the repairs while he went on with his normal life. But, here he was, digging Cheddar's cat carrier out of the garage.

Staring at the crate, Pete wondered if he was making a mistake. Was it fair to take Cheddar away from the home he loved just to be close to Dylan? What if someone left a door open and Cheddar got out? "Shit."

Pete decided to leave the carrier in the garage for now while he sussed out Cheddar's mood. He let himself into the house through the garage. "Kids, I'm home," he called.

When he stepped into the living room he was more than a little surprised to find Cheddar and Julie both sleeping in his recliner. "Well, I guess the two of you have called a truce."

He scooted Julie to the side before lifting the cat into his arms. "Since the two of you seem to have missed me so much, why don't you tell me what's been going on?" He looked at Julie, the innocent one of the two. "Did Cheddar have a party while I was gone?"

Julie opened one droopy eye before moving her chin to rest against Pete's thigh. "Let me guess, Cheddar blackmailed you into keeping your mouth shut in exchange for some companionship. Am I right? Just keep your eyes closed if I am."

When Julie continued her siesta, Pete nodded. "Yeah, that's what I figured." He lifted Cheddar up to eye level. "You're a bad influence."

Cheddar mewed and scrambled out of Pete's arms, leaving behind a thin, bloody scratch. "Don't you get an attitude with me, young man," he scolded, reaching for a tissue.

It was a typical exchange and for some stupid reason it comforted him. It also served to remind him that he was home. He glanced down at Julie. "If only you could use a litter box."

Pete's phone rang, pulling his attention away from the current situation. "Hey."

"You snuck out before I woke up. Does that mean you regret last night?" Dylan asked.

"Far from it. I just have two animals at home that needed me. I think I'm gonna bring Julie over there for the day, but I need to be here at night from now on."

"Oh."

Pete grinned at the disappointment he heard in Dylan's voice. "You're invited, by the way."

"Yeah?"

"Definitely." Pete ran his fingers through his hair. "I just can't give up who I am to clean up David's mess." He rubbed his forehead. "I haven't changed my mind about fixing the house, but this is my home, and I need to remember that."

"Okay, great. Well, I've done a preliminary assessment, and the staircase should be done first, followed by the mantels, then floors and finally the mouldings. The floors can be taken care of by someone else, it'll be faster and cheaper. I'll take some measurements today, but depending on what you want for wood, I'm going to need to order that tomorrow."

"Mahogany," Pete was quick to reply.

"Expensive."

"Yeah, but it's the right material to use. It's what was there before." Pete stood and began to pace. Spending money didn't come easy to him, but in his heart, he didn't think of David's money as his own. It was money to set right a wrong, nothing more. "Listen, you feel like going to the club with me later? I can get you in with a temporary pass from Ray and Mike."

When Dylan didn't reply, Pete continued, "You said it yourself, you have to order the wood tomorrow, so why not get out of there while you can?"

"I wasn't exactly honest with you. I've never worked out anywhere but my garage. I don't know the first thing about using the kind of equipment at a regular health club."

The admission warmed Pete. He doubted Dylan showed the vulnerable side of himself to many people. "We can stick to the free weights, pool and sauna if that makes you feel better."

Dylan chuckled. "Yeah, I think I can handle those."

"Good. I've got a few things to take care of here first. I'll give you my address and you can swing by before we go and meet Cheddar and Julie." Pete received a mew from Cheddar at the mention of his name. He gave Dylan his address before ending the call.

"Yes, I know it's time for you to eat," he said, bending over to run a hand over Cheddar's back. "Don't worry, I won't neglect you again."

* * * *

Dylan pulled into Pete's driveway. The house was small and in need of a new roof, but the landscaping was the best in the neighbourhood. He got out of the pickup and walked up the flower-lined sidewalk. The red front door was like a beacon on the white house with black shutters. *Nice.* Pete definitely had good taste.

Pete opened the door before Dylan had a chance to knock. "Heard you pull up," Pete greeted.

Dylan wasn't sure if he was allowed to touch the man he'd spent the night with or if they were supposed to pretend they were just friends while in public. Pete solved the dilemma by giving Dylan a quick kiss.

"Come on in. I just need to get my bag." Pete led the way into the house before shutting the door behind Dylan.

The moment a fat orange cat spotted Dylan, it gave off a hiss and ran from the room. "Cheddar?"

Pete nodded. "He doesn't do well with strangers, but he'll come around." He pointed to a sleeping white lump in a chair. "That's Julie. She was David's dog." He walked over and gave the bulldog a scratch. "But you're a member of the family now, aren't you, girl?" Pete held up a finger. "I'll be right back."

It was easy to see Pete's affection for the animals, and it made Dylan feel better about Pete's need to relocate to the smaller house. He looked around the room, appreciating what he saw. There was nothing expensive in the room, except maybe the big television, but it was clean and comfortable.

"You're probably wondering why I'd choose this place over the mansion, right?" Pete walked in with athletic shoes in his hand.

"Just the opposite. This place is small, but it's nice." Dylan reached down to pet Julie.

"It's a cracker box held together with duct tape and desperation, but I earned it, I bought it and no one but the bank can take that from me."

The pride in Pete's voice was obvious, prompting Dylan to respect him even more. "Now you'll have the money to get that roof of yours fixed."

"Yeah, and a half dozen other things." Pete finished tying his shoes. "I still have to meet with David's attorney, Matthew Field, this week to talk about the company."

"Any idea what you're going to do?" Dylan asked.

Pete walked over and wrapped his arms around Dylan's waist. "First I'm going to kiss you for a few minutes. After that, I'm taking you to the gym before I bring you back here for takeout Chinese and sex."

Dylan lowered his head. "I like the way you think."

Chapter Four

"Hey, Josh, is Ray or Mike in today?" Pete asked the front desk clerk at the athletic club.

Josh's eyes went wide as he glanced up from the computer and got his first look at Dylan. Yeah, Pete understood his reaction. Dylan was devastating, and the man didn't even seem to know it.

"Uhhh, yeah, I think they're still here," Josh stammered.

Pete snapped his fingers to get Josh's attention. "Can you page one of them for me?"

Josh shook his head in an attempt to focus on the task at hand. He picked up the phone and paged Mike. "If he's here, he'll either call or come to the desk."

"Thanks." Although Pete had been flattered by Josh's obvious attraction to Dylan in the beginning, it was starting to wear on him. "We'll wait for him by the waterfall," Pete told Josh. He took Dylan's hand and led him across the lobby.

"This place is amazing," Dylan said, unaware of the attention his presence had garnered from the men on the second floor.

"Mike's company built it. That's how he met Ray." Pete didn't go into the fact that his ex was currently living with Ray's ex—that was too messy for a first date. He sat on a stone bench in front of the falls.

Dylan continued to wander, looking like an art lover in a gallery. He reached out and caressed the banister of the wide spiral staircase. "Fantastic. You don't see work like this in commercial buildings."

"You do in mine," Mike said, stepping up behind Dylan.

Dylan spun around and smiled. "It's good to see you again."

Mike shook hands with Dylan. "Damn, you get bigger every time I see you." He nodded towards the wall of glass looking down on them. "I've already been asked twice if you're one of the Kansas City Chiefs."

"I've noticed guys checking him out, but I don't think it had anything to do with Dylan possibly being a professional athlete," Pete said, walking over to rest a hand on Dylan's lower back. He glanced up and grinned. *Yeah, motherfuckers, he's mine.*

"Don't pay any attention. People look at me all the time because of my size. Doesn't mean anything," Dylan told Pete.

Although Dylan played off the attention, Pete knew the club was like a meat market. *Hell.* Maybe he'd made a mistake bringing Dylan. It didn't matter that they'd only spent one night together, the thought of losing Dylan like he'd lost Linc was more than he wanted to deal with.

"Ready to work out?" Mike asked.

"I guess so. Pete's promised we can stick with the easy stuff." Dylan smiled down at Pete. "I've never been to a health club," he admitted.

"I can get Manny to show you the equipment if you want?" Mike offered.

An image of the club's Adonis anywhere near Dylan sent warning bells off in Pete's head. "No!" Pete tried to cover the unexpected outburst with a laugh. "I think we'll stick with the weights and pool area today."

Dylan's eyebrows drew together, but he didn't say anything.

"Let's get you set up with a pass. Josh'll have to take your picture, but it should only be a few minutes." Mike led the way to the front counter.

Pete stayed back once they reached it. *What the hell's wrong with me?* Jealousy wasn't an emotion he was comfortable with. Before Linc had played him for a fool, he'd never worried about his partners finding someone else—someone better—but Dylan was hot and fun and...and soooo good in bed.

"I thought you might like him," Mike said, leaving Dylan and Josh to fill out the forms and make the temporary badge.

Pete narrowed his gaze. "You set me up?"

"Not at all. You asked for the best and that's what you got," Mike replied.

"But you left out the part where I'd be hiring the sexiest man I've ever laid eyes on, who, oops, just happens to be gay." Pete glanced at Dylan. "Dammit, Mike, I really like him."

"I can tell." Mike winked. "I don't think Dylan's a player, though, so go easy on the green-eyed monster act."

"But Manny? I can't believe you suggested him." Pete had gone several rounds with Manny and it hadn't ended well, but that didn't mean he thought Manny was any less sexy. "Hell, he can't walk through a room without everyone in it getting hard," Pete said, pleading his case.

Mike's face turned a subtle shade of red. "Happens to the best of us."

"But you have Ray," Pete reminded his friend.

"I also have a cock." Mike shrugged. "I'm also intelligent enough to know it's my body's reaction and not my heart's."

It was different with Pete and Dylan. They didn't love each other. One fuck did not a relationship make. "Maybe once I fall in love again I'll feel the same way, but I've been burned before."

Mike rolled his eyes. "You absolutely cannot blame yourself for Brent and Linc. Brent's a slut who wants what he can't have. I guarantee if he hasn't invited someone else into their bed already, it's coming any time."

Pete knew Brent's fondness for threesomes from his conversations with Mike and Ray, who had started out with Brent. It hadn't ended well between the three of them and they'd almost lost the club because of it.

"Got it," Dylan announced, holding up his newly-laminated Brookside Athletic Club pass. "Josh said he'd find me a lanyard to put it on, but for now I have this little clip thing." He attached the badge to the side of his deep V necked T-shirt.

Mike nudged Pete with his elbow before addressing Dylan, "Come on, I'll show you how to use the equipment."

* * * *

Dylan tried to keep his enthusiasm for all the sleek machines in check. He'd always had a problem admitting his shortcomings to people. He detested looking like a fool. The insecurity had been instilled in him as a child. *Oaf* was a name that had followed him throughout school. Given his size and shy manner, he'd partially understood the comparison, but he was anything but dim witted. To prove it, he'd never attempted anything in school he couldn't excel at. Unfortunately, the pattern had followed him into adulthood.

"Tell me if there's something in particular that catches your eye," Mike said, continuing the tour.

"I know how to walk, so that treadmill doesn't look too difficult, but you'll have to show me how to turn it on and change the gradient." Dylan swallowed around the lump in his throat. "If you don't mind, that is."

Mike gestured for Dylan to climb on. As Mike went through the buttons and their order, Dylan paid close attention, committing the instructions to memory. Once he thought he'd be able to do it again on his own, he stepped off. "Got it."

A deep laugh coming from a few machines over caught Dylan's attention. His hands fisted as he spun around, ready to take on the man laughing at him.

"That's Manny, our head trainer. Pete doesn't want you anywhere near him, though, because he's jealous," Mike announced.

Pete promptly punched Mike in the arm. "Shut up."

Dylan glanced at Pete. "You don't need to worry about Manny."

"Good to know." Pete looked at the heavily muscled trainer. "Because I can't compete with that."

Dylan's attention swung back to the trainer. He was very good-looking, with black hair that hung in a low ponytail between his shoulder blades, an incredibly muscled physique that screamed a lifetime spent in a gym, and brilliant blue eyes that defied his obvious Latin heritage. However, the trainer reminded him of the users he'd come across in his life. Men who were so used to getting what they wanted that they barely took the time to ask. When Manny glanced up and held his gaze, Dylan knew his next move would help determine his chances with Pete. Breaking eye contact, Dylan walked over and gave Pete's forehead a soft kiss. "You don't have to compete with that, believe me."

"There you are," a handsome older man said, wrapping his arms around Mike's waist. "You about ready to get out of here?"

"I thought we were gonna sit in the sauna?" Mike asked.

Ray stood on his toes and whispered something in Mike's ear.

"Oh, shit." Mike suddenly looked uneasy. "I don't suppose we could talk the two of you into going to lunch with us?

Dylan had a feeling the ploy to get them out of the club had something to do with Pete's ex. "Sounds fine to me, but I'll do whatever you want to do," he told Pete.

"Yeah." Pete had obviously figured out Ray's concern as well. He bumped his hip against Dylan. "We'll come back later in the week when it's less crowded."

"Sure," Dylan agreed. The thought of Pete seeing his ex worried him. He didn't know whether or not Pete still had feelings for Linc, but he definitely wasn't prepared to see them if he did.

Dylan followed Mike, Ray and Pete out of the exercise area without giving Manny another look. Instead, his gaze was squarely locked on Pete's ass. Without a workout, they would have even more time in bed.

Win.

* * * *

On the way to the restaurant, Pete knew he needed to say something about what had happened at the club. It had been obvious Dylan had known the reason why Ray and Mike had invited them to lunch, and Pete didn't want Dylan to get the wrong idea.

Pete couldn't believe he'd called Linc less than twenty-four hours earlier. After everything that Linc had done, why in the hell would Pete lower himself to the point of taking the asshole back?

Loneliness.

He glanced at Dylan. That wasn't to say his immediate attraction to Dylan wasn't genuine. It reminded him of that saying, 'happiness finds you when you least expect it'. Yeah, that's exactly what had happened. The big dilemma was whether or not to say something to Dylan about it.

"So, was it just Linc that showed up at the club or did Ray's ex come with him?" Dylan asked without taking his eyes off Mike's truck in front of him.

"I don't know. I didn't see either one of them. I'm assuming it was just Linc because, as far as I know, Brent isn't a member." Pete turned in his seat to face Dylan. "I need you to know something, though."

"Okay."

"Linc hurt me, no doubt about that, but I think it's because our relationship felt unfinished that I continued to think about it." Pete reached over and put a hand on Dylan's thigh. "You told me back at the club that I didn't need to compete with Manny. Well, I can honestly say the same thing to you about Linc."

"Really? 'Cause the way Mike tried to hustle us out of there, I would say the opposite," Dylan replied without looking at Pete.

Shit. Pete unbuckled his seatbelt and scooted across to sit next to Dylan. The two of them weren't really a couple. Hell, they barely knew each other, but he felt good about where they were, which was important to him. "Sometimes people take what they can get because they don't believe they deserve more," he admitted. "You're my more."

Dylan moved his hand from the steering wheel to Pete's leg. "That's probably the nicest thing anyone's ever said to me. I'm not sure I deserve it, but I'd be honoured to work towards being that for you."

Pete rested his head on Dylan's upper arm. "And so you know, I usually don't sleep with a guy until at least the third or fourth date."

Dylan chuckled. "Is that your way of telling me you're not normally a slut?"

"Exactly."

"Well, I've never officially dated anyone, so I guess you could say I am a slut," Dylan confessed.

"Why is that exactly? Is it because of your grandpa?" Pete had never tried to hide who he was, so he didn't understand people who lived with unhappiness in order to accommodate someone else.

Dylan withdrew his hand. "That's one reason, I guess, but I think more than anything, I live in a small town, and I'm not good with opening myself up to criticism. Labels hurt."

Pete found it hard to believe. Dylan seemed pretty damn perfect in his eyes—he was hot, kind and, from what he'd seen, excellent at what he did for a living. "Call me an asshole, but I'm glad you didn't get a chance to fall for someone else."

Dylan pulled into the lot and parked three cars away from Mike. He turned off the engine before leaning over to give Pete a kiss, sweeping his tongue across Pete's before retreating. "I've always been fond of assholes."

Pete burst out laughing. Unable to help himself, he launched himself at Dylan and ended up in the man's lap. It didn't take long to feel the hard length of Dylan's cock against his ass. "And my asshole is fond of you."

Dylan kissed Pete again, his cock growing thicker and harder with each sweep of his tongue. Their impromptu make-out session was interrupted by a knock on the window.

"Are we eating?" Mike asked.

Pete pulled out of the kiss and smiled at Dylan before reaching for the door handle. "You're a natural at this dating thing."

"I'm glad you think so." Dylan helped Pete out of the truck.

"Not a word," Pete warned Mike.

Mike made a show of locking his lips and throwing away the key. His silence didn't last long, though, and before they reached the restaurant, he whispered in Pete's ear, "The two of you are cute together."

Although Mike was bigger by several inches and pounds, Pete easily pushed him off balance. Ray was there to save his partner from tumbling to the pavement, but Pete's point had been made.

* * * *

Dylan finished off his third chilli-cheese hot dog and reached for his fourth. He'd always been a big eater, but from the expressions on Pete, Ray and Mike's faces, they weren't used to one man consuming so much food.

"Amazing," Pete said, leaning his forearms on the table.

Dylan tried to concentrate on his food instead of Pete, but he was still half-hard, and the thought of looking down into those big eyes while he buried his cock was a hell of a lot more important than eating. He set down his dog. "I'm done."

Pete's eyebrows shot up. "Really? You looked pretty hungry a second ago."

If only Pete knew what he was really hungry for. Dylan shook his head. "Naw, I'm good."

"No wonder Pops is still working as old as he is. He probably went into debt trying to feed you as a kid," Mike joked.

Although Dylan knew Mike was teasing, the comment hit a little too close to home. Still, he didn't want to make Mike feel bad, so he played it off. "Why do you think Pops put me to work when I was ten?"

"You ready to get outta here?" Pete asked.

Dylan nodded. "I would imagine it's time to let the dog out."

"Dog? When'd you get a dog?" Ray asked.

"She was David's, but now I think she belongs to Cheddar," Pete explained.

"How is that wild sonofabitch?" Mike chuckled and held out his hand. "See that scar? Cheddar didn't care much for me sitting in Pete's chair when I came over to visit."

"Bullshit. What he didn't care for was you sitting on top of him," Pete countered.

Dylan grinned at the back and forth between the two men. Despite their nearly twenty year age gap, Mike and Pete appeared to be pretty good friends. Other than Pops, Dylan didn't really have anyone he was close to like that. He spoke to his brothers and sister a couple of times a year, but it wasn't much of a conversation beyond checking on each other's health and wishing a *Happy Birthday* or *Merry Christmas*.

Pete got to his feet and stretched his arms over his head. The action brought the bottom of his T-shirt up, giving Dylan a nice flash of skin. Dylan's cock started to harden. *I'm pathetic.* He chalked his overactive libido up to years of depriving himself, but one glance at Pete and he knew the real reason. He'd never wanted someone like he wanted Pete, and while it was scary in some ways, it was also the most exciting time of his life. His skin felt alive when Pete was around, like it was constantly yearning for the slightest touch.

"You want a to-go box for that hot dog?" Pete asked, lowering his arms.

Dylan shook his head. "It's not enough to do anything but make me want more."

Pete moved to squeeze Mike's shoulders, hard if Mike's wince was anything to go by. "We'll see you both later."

Dylan reached out and shook Ray's hand before moving to Mike's. "Good to see you again."

"You, too. Next time you talk to Pops, make sure you tell him I said hi," Mike ordered.

"I will. Depending on how elaborate Pete decides to make the carvings, I could be here for another six months or more. Do you have monthly memberships?" Dylan asked.

"Not for the general public, but for you, sure. Just keep the badge Josh made you, and I'll tell him to activate it as a regular member's pass next time you go in." Mike finished his beer and stood. "Let's go home," he told Ray.

Dylan led the way out of the restaurant, ready to get back to Pete's house. By the time he made it to the truck, his mind was filled with X-rated thoughts that he'd never be able to express aloud. Wanting to run his tongue around the rim of Pete's asshole wasn't something he felt comfortable discussing, but just because he couldn't talk about them didn't mean he didn't want exactly that.

Pete opened the passenger door and immediately started digging between the seats.

"Lose something?" Dylan asked.

Pete pulled his hand out, clutching a seatbelt. "This. I want to sit next to you, but I don't want to get busted for not putting safety first." He climbed in next to Dylan. "This way I'm close enough to touch you."

Dylan wondered if Pete was as aroused as he was. "Where?"

Pete fastened the seatbelt and rested his hand on Dylan's upper thigh. "North or south?"

Dylan grinned. "I thought you wanted to be safe?"

"I am. North or south?"

Wearing only a jock and a pair of warm-up pants, Dylan knew it wouldn't take much for Pete to get to skin. He waited until he'd pulled out of the parking lot before answering. "Northeast."

"Ooh, right to business. I like that in a man." Pete palmed Dylan's growing bulge and started a slow massage. "Inside or outside?"

Dylan swallowed. The thought of innocently driving down the road while Pete jacked him off, set him on fire. "Inside," he ground out between clenched jaws. He gripped the steering wheel tighter and prayed for a few minutes of control as Pete pushed Dylan's jock aside and wrapped his hand around the throbbing erection. "Fuck."

"Get on one of the back roads," Pete instructed.

"I'm not from here, so I don't know the back roads," Dylan admitted.

Pete looked up and around. "Turn right at the light, go three lights down and make a left."

Dylan followed the directions while Pete continued to stroke his cock. He wanted to take his hand off the wheel and touch Pete, but if he did, he'd wreck for sure. Finally making it to the side street, he glanced down at his lap. The sight of Pete's sun-bronzed hand working his cock was more than he could handle without thrusting up. "How much farther?"

"Ten minutes. You'll make a left on Seventy-Ninth Street." Pete unbuckled his seatbelt and scooted his ass towards the door before lowering his head. He ran his closed mouth across the crown of Dylan's cock, painting his lips with pre-cum.

When Pete tilted his chin up and smiled, Dylan almost lost it. "Kiss me," Dylan growled. He took one hand off the wheel to give Pete room to sit up. Pete leaned in and Dylan surprised himself by hungrily licking the tangy pre-cum from his lips. It was yet another first for him, and Dylan wondered how much more there was to learn from Pete.

"You like?" Pete asked.

"You have no idea, but I think any more and I'll forget about driving. Maybe you should stick to a hand job until I get off the roads." Dylan felt his face heat at the request. One thing he liked best about Pete was the way he put him at ease, but that ease he felt would get him in trouble yet.

Pete cupped Dylan's balls and gave them a gentle squeeze. "Your cock is pretty much an award winner. Anyone ever tell you that?"

Dylan liked the way Pete said whatever was on his mind. "I've been called *God* by quite a few men while I had sex with them, but I don't recall any of them giving me a blue ribbon after I came."

"You don't say fuck much, do you?" Pete released Dylan's sac and moved up to squeeze the area just under the head.

"I'm not used to talking like that, I guess, but I'm sure as hell thinking a lot about it since I met you."

"So say it for me?" Pete gathered pre-cum on his thumb and lifted it to his mouth and made a show of licking it off. "Tell me exactly what you're going to do to me once we get back to my place."

Dylan pictured Pete spread out on the mattress and tried to imagine what he'd do if he had free rein over his body. "I'll start with kissing you because I know that gets you horny. Then I'll move down your body, sucking your nipples, your cock and probably end up with my nose buried against your balls."

Pete shoved his free hand down the front of his sweats. "Then what?"

"I'll flip you over so I can run my tongue around that sweet hole of yours, maybe dip inside to touch that velvety-soft skin." Shit, Dylan's talk was about to make him come. He recognised the neighbourhood and realised they were only minutes away from Pete's house. "Once I get you loosened up with my tongue and my fingers, I'll shove my cock into your ass as hard and deep as it'll go."

"Yeah," Pete panted.

"I'll probably give your ass a few heavy-handed slaps as I fuck in and out of you." Dylan had never in his life done half the things he was talking on and on about, but he'd thought of doing them for years. "I'll pull out at the last second and shoot my seed all over your red ass."

With a loud curse, Pete came as Dylan pulled into the driveway. Dylan waited until he'd thrown the truck in park before tilting his head back and bucking up against Pete's fist. His release was powerful and perfect and every other adjective he could think of all rolled into one.

Pete leaned against Dylan's side. "We may need a shower and a short nap before we do all that."

Dylan glanced at the wet spot on the front of Pete's sweats and chuckled. "Yeah, maybe."

Chapter Five

Out of sorts, Pete opened the front door of the Braxton Mansion to an awesome view. Shirtless, Dylan was meticulously carving cherry blossoms into the newel post at the bottom of the staircase. It wasn't the same design that had graced the staircase before, but Dylan had asked for Pete's trust and he'd given it. "Beautiful."

Dylan glanced over his shoulder and smiled. "You like it?"

Pete walked over and ran his hand over Dylan's naked back. "Can you do this with the fireplace mantel in the dining room?"

Dylan turned around on his stool to face Pete. "I can, but I had something else in mind."

After the hard day of work he'd put in, and the meeting with Matthew, Pete needed a little TLC from the man he'd come to rely on. He straddled Dylan's lap and sat down. "I've trusted you this far, might as well go all the way."

Dylan set down his chisel. "How'd your meeting with Matthew go?" He pulled Pete against his chest.

Closing his eyes, Pete rested a cheek on Dylan's chest. He'd come to rely on Dylan's strength and understanding at the end of a bad day, and there seemed to be a lot of those lately. "I told him to sell it to the employees."

"But I thought they couldn't come up with enough backing to meet your price. Are you sure you're ready to do that?" Dylan leant back enough to pull Pete's T-shirt off.

"The sooner I get rid of Braxton Investments, the better. I got a call from one of the local news stations—"

"Which one?" Dylan asked, interrupting Pete.

"What?"

"Which one of the stations?"

"Channel Nine, but that's not the point." Pete had come to expect Dylan's questions. Details seemed to mean a lot to him. From the look of Dylan's work on the newel post, Pete was glad the man paid attention to finer points.

"Cool, that's my favourite." Dylan kissed Pete's forehead. "Sorry. Why'd Channel Nine call you?"

"Because they're running a story on the Braxton employees' bid to keep their jobs in Kansas City. Since I've already got more money than I care to spend, and another three million isn't going to make a lot of difference, I told Matthew to okay the sale." Tired of talking, Pete stood and unfastened his dirty work jeans. He hadn't quit his job, nor did he plan to, but he had been thinking of asking John if they could branch out into landscape design instead of just installation.

Dylan untied Pete's boots. "I love this part of the day." He took off his boots before standing.

Pete pushed his jeans and underwear down and off. "Better than a cold beer after work, that's for sure." He ran his hands over Dylan's bared chest, feeling each dip and ridge of the tight six-pack. In the two months Dylan had been in town, the two of them had fucked at least twice a day, sometimes three or four.

The moment Dylan's erection sprang free, Pete reached for it. He'd learnt every bulging vein when hard and every wrinkle when flaccid. He wondered if it was possible to actually fall in love with a man's cock.

Dylan sat back on his stool and pulled Pete forward. He engulfed the head of Pete's cock in his warm mouth as he gripped Pete's ass.

Pete braced his hands on Dylan's broad shoulders and enjoyed the moment. Oh, fuck, that tongue was talented. Maybe it wasn't just Dylan's cock he'd fallen for — the man's mouth was equally impressive.

"Mmm," Dylan moaned around the cock in his throat.

"Yeah," Pete agreed. He began a slow, shallow thrust. Each time Dylan tried to take more of Pete's length, Pete pulled back, keeping Dylan's attention to the head and a few inches. One thing Pete had learnt about his new lover was what drove him crazy. Denying Dylan what he really wanted seemed to work every time.

With a grunt, Dylan eased off Pete's cock and stared up at him. "Condom. Now."

Pete turned around and bent over to retrieve one of the packets and the bottle of lube Dylan kept in his toolbox. He purposely kept his knees locked in an effort to give Dylan a good look at what he would soon be fucking.

"Now that's just like waving a red cape in front of a bull," Dylan gruffed.

Pete handed Dylan the lube. "You can eat my ass later all you want, but for now, I'm in the mood for that cock of yours." He glanced over his shoulder. "If that's okay with you?"

Dylan dripped the slick down the crack of Pete's ass before pushing a finger inside. "Unwrap the goddamn rubber and hand it back," he instructed.

Grinning like a fool, Pete gave Dylan what he wanted. Dylan, with a dash of anger, was a beautiful thing. Pete knew he was in for one hell of a fuck, and after the day he'd had, he was more than ready.

Dylan stood and pushed Pete over to the newel. "Hold on."

Pete felt the carvings under his palms as he gripped the post.

"I'm done stretchin'. You're gonna feel every inch of my dick."

"Counting on it, babe." Pete had never been the kind of guy to give stupid pet names to past lovers, but Dylan's heart was so pure and innocent — when he wasn't fucking the shit out of Pete — the nickname fit him to a T.

Dylan answered by pushing the crown of his sheathed cock into Pete's hole.

Thankfully, their regular sessions had prepared Pete for the long, fat cock that drove in deep.

"You feel me?" Dylan asked.

"I do." Pete stared down at his cock. It needed attention, but if he took a hand off the post, he'd finish the fuck with cherry blossom impressions all over his forehead.

"Need your hand," Pete said, pushing back against Dylan's dick.

Dylan slapped Pete's ass several times.

Pete loved it when Dylan set his ass on fire with the palm of his hand, but... "Feels good, but I was talking about my cock. It needs some attention."

Dylan grabbed Pete's hips and pulled him back a few steps. "Stretch out on the floor. Careful of the chisel."

Oddly touched by Dylan's concern, Pete laid down. Despite Dylan's natural instincts to master, he also showed how much he cared about Pete's safety.

"There," Dylan said once he'd put a rolled up pair of jeans under Pete's head. "Now you can jerk off while I get back to business." He slapped Pete's ass several more times before smoothing his hand across the reddened skin. "This sure is pretty."

Pete wrapped his hand around his cock. The tingling he felt at Dylan's gentle touch pushed him closer to the edge. No doubt Dylan would spend the rest of the evening kissing and applying salve to Pete's ass to make up for his momentary loss of control. It was Pete's favourite part. He never thought he was the kind of man who needed to be cared for, but Dylan had a way of showing Pete all kinds of things he hadn't known he needed.

Dylan thrust in deep and swivelled his hips, grinding himself against Pete's sensitive skin. The scratch of Dylan's short pubes against him added another level of prickly pleasure, hurtling Pete to climax. "Fuuuckkk!"

Dylan applied another slap, prolonging Pete's orgasm. "My ass," Dylan proclaimed, bucking several times as he came.

Pete nodded. Yeah, Dylan had truly taken possession of his ass and heart. Perhaps he'd have to think of a few more projects around the Braxton Mansion for Dylan to do.

* * * *

Dylan set two plates of goulash on the coffee table. "You need another beer?"

Naked, with a pillow under his groin and his ass in the air, Pete looked up from a sales circular from the Sunday paper and shook his head. "I'm fine."

Dylan went back into the kitchen and retrieved a dishtowel and two ice packs. He wasn't sure what was bothering Pete, but he aimed to find out because the fear that he had really hurt Pete during their after work playtime was weighing heavily on his heart. He set the supplies on the sofa and held out his hand.

Pete put the paper aside and reached for Dylan's offered hand. "Thanks. My ass stings a little more than usual tonight."

Dylan quickly put the dishtowel down followed by the ice packs, and finally the thin pillow. He helped ease Pete back on the couch. "I'm sorry. I didn't mean to get so carried away." He sat next to Pete. "I swear, I'll never do it again."

Pete handed Dylan a plate. "Don't say that. I like what you do to me, all of it."

"So why're you so upset with me?" Dylan asked. He looked at his dinner and decided he no longer had an appetite.

Pete took the plate out of Dylan's hands and set it back on the table before moving to kneel between his legs. "I'm not upset with you at all."

"Then why aren't you talking to me?" Dylan cupped Pete's face. "Whatever I've done, I can't fix it if you don't tell me what it is."

"I'm falling in love with you," Pete announced. "And those feelings are usually followed by heartbreak, and I'm not ready for that."

Dylan gathered Pete up and lifted him onto his lap. Pete's answer wasn't at all what he'd expected to hear. "Falling in love is a good thing, right?"

"Sure, if it works, but for me it never does."

Dylan rested his hand on the still-heated welts on Pete's ass. He understood why Pete felt the way he did. Pete hadn't had the best luck when it came to people standing by him, but Dylan liked to believe he was different. "I'm still here."

"For now," Pete mumbled.

"I fell in love that first week I was in town, and I haven't gone anywhere." Dylan tilted Pete's chin up and gave him a deep kiss. It had been the first time he'd shared his true feelings. He hadn't intended to confess his love until the time was right and all Pete's outside problems had been resolved, but he realised, Pete's needs came first.

"What happens when the house's finished?"

"That's months away. You might be tired of me by then," Dylan said. He'd tried not to worry about what would happen once the Braxton Mansion was completed, but not for the reason Pete thought.

"It's not possible to get tired of someone who can fuck and cook like you do." Pete slid off Dylan's lap and onto the pillow. "Eat, before it's cold."

Dylan wasn't sure what had just happened. "That's it?"

"For now." Pete took a bite of goulash. "And I'll give you reasons to stay after dinner."

Dylan gathered food onto his fork. Pete didn't have to do anything but continue to be the man he'd grown to know since that first night, but he wouldn't tell Pete that, yet.

* * * *

Dylan entered the athletic club and swiped his card. "Evening, Josh."

Josh's face lit up in a brilliant smile. "Hey, I haven't seen you around much lately."

"Yeah, I've been busy, but Pete's having dinner with his boss, so I thought I'd come and get a workout in before going home." Dylan stuffed his identification card back into his gym bag. "See ya later."

"Hope so," Josh added as Dylan headed for the locker room.

Dylan nodded a greeting to several men as he passed, making sure to keep his gaze above their waists. It was his first time at the club on his own, and although he'd become comfortable with the layout, the meat-market vibe of the place was a drawback for him. Before meeting Pete, Dylan would've killed for a place where he could be open and honest about who he was and what he wanted from another man, but things had changed and his cock might as well have a reserved sign hung on it.

Finding an open locker towards the back of the room, Dylan set his bag on the bench and started to undress. Moans filled the back corner, drawing his attention to the large communal shower space. As tempted as he was to investigate, he decided to mind his own business.

As he searched for his jock, the grunts and moans grew louder, but again, he tried to ignore it. He was in the process of fitting his jock in place when it happened, the unmistakable sound of a hand slapping against wet skin. *Shit.*

Dylan's cock started to harden, making it difficult to capture his length in the jock's pouch. The moans got even louder as more slaps landed. *Fuck!* Dylan grabbed a towel from the rack beside the lockers and wrapped it around his waist.

Dylan entered one of the toilet stalls and hung his towel on the hook before taking himself in hand.

A voice deeper than Dylan's said something in Spanish before another loud smack sounded.

Dylan jacked his cock with one hand while cupping and squeezing his balls with the other. His need for Pete had never been stronger than at that moment. He'd been worried that he was perverse for the things he'd done to Pete and the things he still wanted to do, but evidently he wasn't alone in his unique needs.

A deep grunting sound filled the locker room, pushing Dylan over the edge. His first strand of seed splashed against the closed door in front of him, quickly followed by several more volleys until his balls were emptied, making a mess of the door and floor.

By the time he'd caught his breath and had wrapped the towel around his waist again, the shower had turned off. Dylan waited for several seconds before opening the stall door.

Leaning against the wall with his arms crossed over his muscular chest was Manny. Christ, Dylan should've known it had to be him. Manny met Dylan's gaze and smiled. "You should join in next time."

Knowing he'd been caught, Dylan squared his shoulders. Unless he wanted to be intimidated by Manny for the rest of his time in Kansas City, he needed to set the gorgeous man straight on a few things. He walked over to stand in front of Manny. "Only if you like the feel of a big cock shoved up your ass."

Manny laughed. The genuine sound surprised Dylan. "Fair enough," Manny said. "But you can also come in and watch. No need to hide what I assume is an impressive dick behind a closed door."

Dylan looked around for whoever Manny had just fucked, but they were alone in the locker room. He decided to use the opportunity instead of running away. "I like to spank my partner while I fuck him, too. There's just something about the way the skin gets hot under my hand that gets me off." He shrugged. "I wasn't always like that, not until I met Pete."

Manny chuckled, flashing brilliant white teeth. "Branding. You want to make sure he can feel your touch for hours after you've fucked him."

Despite Dylan's first impression of the trainer, he suddenly felt he'd met a kindred spirit. "Yeah. That's exactly it."

"Get dressed, and I'll spot you on the free weights," Manny offered.

"Sure, but I figured you were done for the day." Dylan walked over to the bench and finished getting dressed.

"Why, because I took a shower?" Manny slipped on a pair of shorts without bothering with underwear or a jock. No doubt his usual clients enjoyed the thought of Manny freeballing.

"Yeah." Dylan bent over to tie his shoes.

"I take a shower after each of my personal clients." He winked. "Some of them require more work than others."

Dylan shoved his clothes and bag into the locker. "So, am I to assume you just finished with a client?"

Manny licked his lips. "What can I say? I'm damn good at giving that something extra that most trainers don't."

Dylan couldn't imagine the number of men Manny fucked in a day. "Sounds like something I would've enjoyed before I met Pete."

"But not now?" Manny questioned, leading the way out of the locker room.

"No. I've found everything I've ever wanted, so why fuck it up?" Dylan entered the weight room and immediately went to the back corner. It was a bench set-up that he'd used before and made him feel comfortable because it was the farthest away from the viewing window as he could get.

Without asking, Manny began to load weights onto the bar. "You're lucky, you know that?"

"Yeah, I do. What about you, don't you get tired of fucking someone different all the time, or is it a matter of money?" *Fuck.* Dylan couldn't believe he'd actually said that. "Sorry. Don't answer that."

"Don't get all shy on me now. Hell, you just listened to me fuck a guy." Manny checked the weights. "You okay with this?"

"It'll do for a warm-up." Dylan straddled the narrow bench and laid back. He tested his grip on the bar before nodding to Manny.

"Just so you know, I don't get paid for the fucking," Manny said as he continued to spot Dylan.

"Like I said, it's none of my business, and I shouldn't have asked." Dylan set the weight bar back into its cradle. "Put another twenty on both sides."

"Here's the thing. I can fuck all day, every day, and never get tired of it, but if I fuck the same guy too many times, he starts thinking there's more to the relationship than there really is. The only answer I've been able to find is to spread myself around."

"There you are," Pete said, walking over. He glanced suspiciously from Dylan to Manny. "What's going on?"

Dylan remembered Pete's obvious insecurity about Manny that first day, and hoped he could put his love at ease, but he knew in order to do that, he would need a moment alone. "Thanks for your help, Manny, but Pete can take it from here."

Manny gave Dylan an understanding grin. "Catch you later. I'll be next door if you need anything."

Dylan waited until he and Pete were alone before crooking his finger. "Lean down here and kiss me."

"Not until you tell me why the two of you looked so damn cosy."

Dylan reached for the towel by his head and wiped the sweat from his brow. "I told you before, I have no desire to fuck that man." He didn't tell Pete that he'd listened to Manny fuck another guy, but he would. *Eventually.*

"So why were you in here with him?" Pete asked, taking Manny's position at the bar.

"Because he's a nice guy. We started talking, and I told him I had no desire to be with anyone but you, he said fine then asked if I needed a spotter." Dylan made no move to lift the weights. "I did about twenty reps then you came in." He sat up and spun around on the bench until he faced Pete. "So why're you here so early? Didn't your dinner with John go well?"

"John got called away by an emergency," Pete said. He moved around the set of weights and sat on the bench in front of Dylan. "My heart nearly stopped when I saw the two of you together."

Dylan pulled Pete closer until Pete's legs draped over his. "I want to fuck you. Right here. Right now."

Pete's eyebrows shot up. He climbed on Dylan's lap. "What's gotten in to you?"

Dylan knew it was time to come clean with what he'd done and why. "When I was getting dressed, I heard two guys fucking in the shower. I tried my best to ignore it, but then one of the men started spanking the other one." He closed his eyes and grinned. "Damn, I can't tell you what that sound did to me. I had no choice but to go into one of the stalls and jack off."

With his arms draped over Dylan's shoulders, Pete started to grind his ass against Dylan's cock. "And let me guess, Manny was the one doing the fucking?"

"Yeah, but I didn't know that at the time. It wasn't about the men. It was the sounds, and who they made me think of." Dylan squeezed Pete's ass. "I can't tell you what's going on with me, but I've got all these thoughts in my head about things I want to do to you."

"So what's stopping you?" Pete reached between them and shoved his hand down the front of Dylan's shorts.

Dylan rested his forehead against Pete's shoulder as he was given an expert hand job. He didn't deserve a man like Pete. "I love you."

Several loud men in their twenties came into the room, breaking the moment. Dylan stared into Pete's eyes. "We'd better get out of here."

"Why?" Pete continued to stroke Dylan's cock without missing a beat. He'd never fucked in front of an audience, but the moment the other members had entered the room, he'd noticed a remarkable difference in Dylan's erection. He lifted his hand and sucked the pre-cum from the backs of his fingers. Dylan may not be aware of it, but he wanted this.

Dylan nodded towards the other men. "They'll see."

"If you don't want them in here while I finish you off, tell 'em to leave."

Dylan's gaze shifted back and forth between Pete and the men who were currently looking in their direction. "It might be different if I knew them, but I don't."

"Why don't you boys go find somewhere else to play?" Pete ordered.

"And why don't the two of you go the fuck home and do that shit?" one of the men replied.

With a growl, Dylan stood and turned to face them. "Say that again?" Three sets of eyes bulged as they witnessed the full scope of Dylan's size. "Now, I believe you were told to get the fuck out."

The three men left without another word, but Pete could tell by their expressions that they were pissed off. He didn't blame them for being angry—it was a weight room not a bathhouse—but he had a point to prove to Dylan and nothing and no one would keep him from finishing off the man he loved.

Pete scooted back on the bench and pushed the waistband of Dylan's shorts down below his balls. "Relax."

Dylan braced his arms on the bench behind him and leant back. "We're so getting kicked out of here."

Pete touched his tongue to the base of Dylan's cock and worked his way up, licking the pre-cum as he went. Reaching the head, Pete slipped his lips over the crown and sucked. When Dylan's hand landed on the back of his head, Pete braced himself for what he knew was coming.

"Suck it," Dylan said, fucking Pete's mouth.

Pete moved his hand down to grip Dylan's balls as he opened his throat to Dylan's thrusts. When he'd entered the weight room, he hadn't planned to give Dylan head in such a public place, but after the scene he'd walked in on, he wanted to make sure every member of the club knew who Dylan belonged to. If his suspicion was right, half the men in the next room already knew what was going on only a few feet away from them.

Good.

Dylan's hold on Pete's hair tightened as the first spurt of creamy goodness hit the back of Pete's throat. Pete did his best to swallow every drop before pulling back. He sat up and reached up to wipe his mouth.

"Stop. Let me." Dylan leaned in and licked the spilled cum from Pete's chin.

Pete felt his face heat as he realised they had an audience. Manny stood in the doorway, rubbing the front of his shorts. "Is there a problem?" Pete asked.

"Not from what I could see," Manny said. "Although there's a group of guys that would really like a chance to finish their circuit training. You do know we have a VIP area downstairs for that sorta thing?"

"Shut up, Manny." Despite Dylan's belief that Manny was a good guy, Pete knew the truth. Unbeknownst to Dylan, for a few short weeks after Linc had walked out on him, Pete had been on the receiving end of Manny's insatiable sex drive. Things had gone great until Pete had made the unforgivable mistake of asking Manny out on a real date. A few days later, he'd caught Manny fucking a businessman in his car.

"I'll wait for you downstairs," Pete told Dylan before walking towards the door. He stood in front of Manny and stared the good-looking sonofabitch in the eyes. "He's mine."

"Yes, he's made that very clear to me already," Manny replied. He leant down and whispered in Pete's ear. "The only thing I want from him is friendship, I assure you."

"Just make sure you don't screw him over," Pete added.

"I'm not proud of what happened between us, but I told you in the beginning not to get attached."

"Is there a problem?" Dylan asked.

Pete continued to stare at Manny. One thing Pete knew about Manny was that he didn't lie, not even to save someone's feelings, so Pete believed him when he said he only wanted friendship from Dylan. "No problem."

Dylan shook Manny's hand. "Sorry if we caused a problem for you with those guys."

Manny stepped back out of the doorway. "Don't worry about it. You probably gave them good jerk-off material for the next week." He left Pete and Dylan alone and went back to work.

"Let's get out of here," Dylan said, wrapping his arm around Pete. "We can get some drive-thru on the way home."

"Sounds like a plan."

Chapter Six

Pete stood at the end of the driveway and surveyed the mansion's landscaping. He'd worked for months to restore the flowerbeds and the grand rose garden in the centre of the circle drive. His heart sank as he thought of all the work he'd put in. It wasn't that the gardens weren't beautiful, but looking at them didn't bring him the same peace they used to.

Disgusted, he started up the drive towards the house. He pulled out his phone and made a call.

"Hey," John answered.

"Are you busy?" Pete stopped under one of the grand oak trees and adjusted the spray on one of the underground sprinkler heads.

John sighed. "No, just in the doghouse, as usual. What's up?"

"I hate to ruin your Saturday, but I finished the landscaping at the mansion, and it doesn't look right to me. Would you mind stopping by sometime today?"

"Hell, the way the day's shaping up around here, I'd be happy to get away for a while. Give me an hour."

"Thanks." Pete hung up. John seemed to be arguing with Paula a lot lately. He'd known the couple for years, and although they had disagreements like all couples, they usually worked things out fairly quickly. Unfortunately, for almost three months John seemed to constantly be in a bad mood because of problems at home.

The thwarted dinner Pete had tried to set up with John to discuss branching out into landscape design, had fallen through because Paula had called just as they'd sat down. John had left in a rush and had refused to talk about it afterwards.

Pete entered the house and stopped to appreciate the finished staircase. There were differences between the one from his childhood and the masterpiece Dylan had painstakingly created, but he admitted he liked Dylan's more.

"Pete?" Dylan called.

"Yeah." Pete found Dylan in the dining room. He held his dirty hands up. "I haven't had a chance to wash up."

Dylan grabbed one of Pete's hands and pulled him down for a kiss. "Dirt doesn't scare me." He gestured to the fireplace surround. "What do you think?"

Garlands of perfectly detailed fruits were draped from a centre medallion of a carved sheaf of wheat. Pete tried to remember what the fireplace had looked like before, but he couldn't picture it.

Dylan squeezed Pete's hand. "You don't like it."

Pete shook his head. "No... I mean, yes, I love it."

Dylan tugged on Pete's hand until Pete gave up and sat on the floor. "So what's going on?"

Pete wasn't sure how to put his feelings into words, but he knew he owed Dylan an explanation. "I'm starting to figure out that I can't recreate the home I grew up in."

"Because of the work I'm doing? I can start over if you want—no extra charge. The important thing is that you're happy with the end result." Dylan didn't look at Pete as he made the offer.

"Your work is absolutely beautiful, and the changes you've made are definitely for the better. The problem's with me." Pete felt himself getting emotional, something he rarely did, even in front of Cheddar.

Dylan sat up, moved his stool out of the way and sat on the floor beside Pete. "It's okay," he said, wrapping his arms around Pete.

"No, it's not. I honestly believed restoring the house would give me back what I'd lost, but I'm figuring out the home I grew up in had nothing to do with the house. Does that make sense?" Pete pressed his face against Dylan in an attempt to hide the tears that were dangerously close to falling.

"Of course it does." Dylan kissed the top of Pete's head. "Hang on. There's something I want to show you." He released Pete and got to his feet. Walking over to his makeshift design table, Dylan retrieved two stacks of pictures. "These are the photos you gave me when I first started." He handed one of them to Pete as he sat back down.

"Yeah." Pete didn't need to look at the pictures, he'd already memorised them.

Dylan handed over the other stack. "And these are the photos I took out of the album."

Pete looked through the second stack. "Okay."

Dylan used a rag to clean the dust from an area of the floor before laying all the pictures out. "What's the difference between these?"

It took Pete a moment to see it, but when he did, everything became clear. "The ones I gave you all have either my mom or my brother in them, and the ones you found show more of the actual woodwork."

"Mmm hmm," Dylan agreed.

"I've been trying to recreate my family instead of the house," Pete surmised.

"Yeah."

"So where does that leave me?" Pete asked.

"Sorting things out." Dylan scooped up the pictures and carried them back to their place on his table. "I want to finish the job. Not to give you the home you lost, but to give this house back its soul."

Pete swallowed several times, trying to keep his emotions at bay once again. Dylan's truth was a special gift, and Pete hoped he never took it for granted. He thought of the flowerbeds he'd worked so hard on and came to the same conclusion. "I should probably call John again. I asked him to come over and tell me what I'd done wrong in the gardens, but I think I just got my answer."

"The flowerbeds are gorgeous," Dylan argued.

"Yeah, I guess so." Pete stood and stretched his arms over his head. "I'm gonna let you get back to work."

Dylan gave Pete a deep kiss before landing a playful swat on his ass. "Find me when you're ready to go."

"Absolutely." Pete couldn't imagine going home without Dylan, which continued to worry him. After another deep kiss he made his way back through the house to the front steps. Dylan had been right, the beds were gorgeous.

He pulled out his phone, ready to make the call to his boss when he spotted John's white truck pulling in through the open gates. When John parked, Pete threw up a hand in greeting. "Hey."

Dressed in a thin white muscle shirt and faded pair of ripped jeans, John climbed out of the pickup and stared at the rose garden. "Looks good to me."

Pete joined his boss and best friend. "Yeah, I was going to call and tell you not to bother coming over, but you got here before I had a chance."

John took off walking, leaving Pete no choice but to follow. "You did me a favour, so don't worry about it." He crossed the lawn to the first mixed bed.

Pete never knew whether or not he was supposed to ask his best friend personal stuff, but John seemed upset. "Feel like talking about it?"

John tore his gaze away from the impatiens. "Paula thinks I'm cheating on her."

Wow. That was the last thing Pete had expected to hear. "That's crazy."

When John didn't agree right away, Pete added, "Isn't it?"

"Depends on what you consider cheating," John said. "I haven't had sex with anyone, but I've been talking to people online from my computer at work."

Pete had a hard time imagining John huddled over a computer keyboard, sharing his fantasies with strangers. "So...have you talked to anyone special?"

John rubbed the back of his neck, drawing attention to the tattoos on his arms and shoulder blade.

"You don't have to answer that," Pete was quick to add.

"No, that's okay, it's just not something I've ever actually admitted out loud." John squatted and picked up a handful of the dark coco shell mulch Pete had decided to use. "Remember when I told you that I hired you because I saw something of myself in you?"

"Yeah?"

"Well… Fuck!" John walked away without finishing the sentence. He stood with his hands on his hips, staring up at one of the century-old trees. "I've been talking to men."

Pete almost swallowed his tongue at the confession. A new image of John jacking off for someone over the webcam on the office computer assaulted him. He scrubbed at his eyes to dispel the thought. "Okay, so, are you saying you're bi or gay?"

"I don't know. I've fucked Paula for years, and it didn't make me want to throw up or anything, but lately I've been feeling the other side of me." In his lower forties, it was possible John was experiencing nothing more than a mid-life crisis, but guys hitting that wall usually went out and got a sports car, not another cock to play with.

"Hmm, bi, I reckon," Pete finally decided. "What're you going to do about it, or have you decided?"

"I don't know, but Paula's about to take the decision out of my hands."

"I'm not the best at giving advice, but I think you should tell her the truth." Pete held his breath, hoping he hadn't just wrecked his friendship.

"I love her," John said. "I just don't think I'm *in* love with her anymore. If I tell her the truth, it'll really hurt her."

Pete shrugged. "From what you've said, she's hurting now. At least she'll know the truth. She'll have a reason to feel like she does." Damn, look at him being all grown-up. A thought occurred to him. "Hey, out of curiosity, are you attracted to me?"

John spun around. "Excuse me?"

"It's okay if you are," Pete tried to put him at ease.

"I'm not."

Pete was offended. "Why not? I'm a damn good looking guy."

"You're also, like, my son," John argued.

John wasn't old enough to be his father, but Pete understood the comparison. "I like to think of you as my best friend, but yeah, you did teach me what it meant to be a man."

John walked over and slung an arm over Pete's shoulders. "You are a good-looking sonofabitch though."

"Thank you, I appreciate the recognition." Pete bumped John with his hip. "Let me know when you're ready, and I'll help you navigate the treacherous waters of gaydom."

"Deal."

* * * *

Dylan watched Pete and John inspect the flowerbeds from his position in front of the large picture window in the living room. It was easy to see the camaraderie between the two men, and, if he wasn't mistaken, love.

He wondered when Pete would understand that he may have lost the family he'd once had, but that didn't mean he was without people who truly cared about him. When John wrapped his arm around Pete, Dylan didn't feel a moment of jealousy. Although he'd met John on only a couple of occasions, he didn't know much about the man except that he'd helped Pete when he'd needed it the most. That was enough in Dylan's book to trust him.

The conversation with Pete about the house hadn't been an easy one, but Dylan had been trying to figure out how to talk to him about it for months. Now that the truth was out there, maybe Pete could start to heal.

Dylan turned away from the window, then walked back to the dining room and picked up his phone. He'd made it a habit to call Pops once a day to check on him, much to his grandpop's irritation.

"Afternoon, D," Pops answered.

"How'd you know it was me?" Dylan leaned his hand against the mantel and stared at the work he'd done earlier in the day.

"You're the only one who ever calls." Pops chuckled. "So how's it coming?"

"Good. I think you'd be real proud of the fireplace surround I'm working on. I'll have to take some pictures and send them to you," Dylan offered.

"Real pictures. In the real mail. None of that computer stuff."

Dylan grinned. "I will. So tell me what else's going on?"

"You've lived here long enough to know nothing goes on in this town. That's why I like it. Your mom called yesterday after I talked to you. Said James has been sick and asked if I had anything to tide them over until he could get back to work."

Dylan rolled his eyes. His father was worthless whether he was sick or not. "You didn't give 'em anything, did you?"

"Not much, just a couple hundred, but I told her that's all I had."

Dylan hated that Pops had given them anything, but the old man was crafty. He reckoned Pops had at least a hundred thousand in the attic and probably more stuffed in every cubbyhole in the house. Like almost everything in the world, Pops didn't trust banks of any kind. "Good thinking. Next time Mom calls, tell her if she wants money to call me."

"You're not going to…"

"Heck no," Dylan replied, watching his language. "I'm going to tell her exactly what I think of her for asking, though."

"You're such a good boy." Pops chuckled.

"Thanks. I'll call ya tomorrow?"

"I'll be here." Pops hung up without saying goodbye. *Typical.*

Dylan set the phone down before he did something rash like call his mom and chew her a new asshole for bothering Pops. Unfortunately, he knew it wouldn't do any good. His mom and dad had leached off Pops, the system and any church dumb enough to help them for years.

Dylan kicked at the stool, sending it flying across the room. His parents had dropped him off at Pops and Grandmom's house when he was two weeks old, claiming he was too much to take care of, and Dylan had been with Pops since that day. Even after his biological parents had their shit halfway together, they hadn't tried to get Dylan back. Instead, they'd had more children. The only time they'd cared enough to ask about Dylan had been when they'd needed money.

He'd grown up ten miles from siblings he'd barely known, and had never once been invited over to his parents' house for a holiday gathering or birthday party.

Fuck. Them.

Dylan refused to allow the hatred he felt for his mom and dad invade the peace he'd found with Pete. He walked over and retrieved the stool from the other side of the room and righted it once more. Staring at the work in front of him, he decided to stop for the day. A house built in anger was a house cursed.

Decision made, Dylan put his tools away, making sure to wipe each one clean before fitting it in the old, velvet-lined chest. Finished, he went in search of the one man guaranteed to lift his spirits.

Dylan was surprised to find John's truck gone from the driveway. He scanned the lawn and spotted Pete leaning against one of the stone and mortar fence posts that surrounded the property.

Instead of traipsing across the lawn, Dylan turned around and went back into the house. He jogged up the staircase and entered David's old bedroom. "Ready to go home?" he asked, lifting Julie into his arms. "I think our boy could use a nice evening of family time."

* * * *

After John had left, Pete wandered the yard until he found himself sitting with his back against the cool stone of one of the pillars. It was a good place to take a deep breath and study the Braxton Mansion for what it was—real estate.

He watched as Dylan came out of the house and lifted Julie into the truck. Pete pulled out his phone and checked the time. It was only two. Usually Dylan worked until at least five on Saturdays. Pete walked to the driveway and waited for Dylan to reach him.

"Hey, Julie and I are ready to go home. Interested?" Dylan asked.

"Absolutely." Pete opened the door and climbed in. He couldn't wait to get away from the mansion. Dylan had been right. He needed to figure a few things out and he couldn't do it surrounded by the past.

Dylan hit the remote to close the gates as soon as the tailgate cleared them. "I thought we could stop by Redbox and pick up a couple of movies."

Pete nodded in agreement and continued to play with Julie's soft, floppy ears. "John's bisexual," he blurted out.

"What?"

"Yeah, he told me today. Well, to be honest, he said he didn't know what he was, except he still enjoyed fucking his wife, although he's been talking to guys online." Pete glanced at Dylan. "I had no idea. My gaydar never once went off around him."

"Turn in your gay card," Dylan said with a straight face.

"Over my dead body." Pete returned his attention to Julie. "I think I'm going to take a break from the mansion for a while, if you don't mind?"

Dylan reached over and rubbed the back of Pete's neck. "Not at all. Take the time you need."

"It's just that I wanna finish things up with Matthew, get some work done on the house and finally pin John down long enough to discuss the expansion idea—"

"You don't have to defend yourself to me," Dylan said, cutting Pete off. "I'll continue to work during the day and come by your place when I'm done if that's okay?"

"I'd be crushed if you didn't. I've come to rely on you being there at the end of the day." Pete knew he could be setting himself up for quite a fall if Dylan decided to go back to Maine after the job, but he'd decided weeks ago he wasn't going to hold back.

"Good, because I've begun to think of your house as home."

"I'm glad you feel that way." Pete thought about the narrow shower and tiny kitchen in his place. It had always been fine for one person, but things were tight with two. Short term wasn't a problem, but if he somehow managed to convince Dylan to stay, they'd be tripping over each other come winter. The mansion was definitely out of the question. Which left only two options—move or expand the square footage of his house. "Tell me about the house you grew up in?"

"It's the same house I still live in with Pops. Nothing special." Dylan glanced at Pete. "Two bedroom craftsman-style with the prettiest woodwork you've ever seen. The outside hasn't seen a paintbrush in years, but that's the way Pops likes it."

"Why's that?" Pete asked. There was still a lot about Dylan's home life that he didn't know.

"Because according to Pops, flaunting what you have, while surrounded by those doing without, is a sin." Dylan chuckled. "My saving grace as a boy was a little fishing hole about a mile down the road."

"I didn't know you liked to fish." Pete noticed that Julie was starting to pant and adjusted the air vent to blow on her.

"Love it. You don't grow up in Maine without learning to fish." Dylan pulled into a grocery store parking lot. "You fish?"

"Me? No. I didn't have that kind of father."

Dylan opened his door. "You've been grown for several years now. If you'd wanted to learn to fish, you could've taught yourself by now."

Before Pete could answer, Dylan was jogging across the lot towards the Red Box in front of the store. Pete didn't worry about what movies Dylan would pick out. They both enjoyed action or comedies.

As he watched Dylan go through the available movies, Pete thought about Dylan's last comment. He supposed Dylan was right. He could no longer blame his father for his shortcomings.

Dylan was all smiles when he made it back to the truck. "We lucked out." He held up all three Transporter movies. "It's a Jason Statham marathon."

Pete liked that the little things in life made Dylan happy. Of course, he also knew what a crush Dylan had on the action star, which was a win for Pete because they'd no doubt get to fuck between each movie. "Excellent."

* * * *

With a hand towel slung over his shoulder, a bowlful of ice in one hand and popcorn in the other, Dylan entered the bedroom. "I used the last bag of popcorn."

Lying on his stomach with his red ass propped up on a pillow, Pete glanced over his shoulder. "Did you put it on the list?"

"No, but I will. I had other things on my mind." Dylan set the popcorn down towards the end of the mattress next to Pete's elbow.

"Don't forget or you'll be grouchy next time we watch a movie." Pete pushed the play button on the remote.

Dylan put a few more pillows under Pete's groin. "Scoot your knees up under the pillow." The new position put Pete's ass in the air. "Comfortable?" Dylan asked.

Pete tossed a few kernels into his mouth and nodded without taking his eyes off the TV.

Before soothing the reddened skin with the ice, Dylan couldn't resist feeling the hot flesh against him. He rested the side of his head against one of Pete's ass cheeks and lazily drew his finger up and down the crack. They'd started fucking bareback a couple of weeks earlier, after being tested, and Dylan loved the way his cum felt on Pete's skin. He pushed his finger into Pete's stretched hole. "I'll never get tired of this," he mumbled to himself.

Pete clenched, momentarily trapping Dylan's finger. "Should I put the movie on pause?"

"No, I'm just playing." Dylan moved to sit directly behind Pete's kneeling body and reached for the bowl of ice. With a cube in each hand, Dylan gently ran his palms over the red welts.

"Mmmm, nice," Pete moaned.

Dylan separated the cheeks of Pete's ass and licked the sticky cum still clinging to Pete's hole. He'd fucked Pete for the second time only fifteen minutes earlier, but his cock was already getting hard again. That's the way it was between them. They could be doing something as mundane as washing the dishes and one look or movement from Pete could make Dylan hard in seconds.

Dylan had discovered the beauty in privacy. Knowing they were free to fuck whenever the mood struck was a huge aphrodisiac. In the beginning of their relationship, Dylan thought it was the newness of it all that had him horny all the time, but he'd come to the realisation that his desire to fuck Pete only grew stronger by the day.

"Lube's back on the table," Pete said, pushing his ass against Dylan's face.

"Not yet," Dylan replied, pulling back. He reached for another ice cube and rimmed Pete's hole with it.

"Fuck!" Pete reached under himself and wrapped a hand around his cock.

"If you liked that, you're going to love this." Dylan popped the cube into Pete's ass and held it there using his fingers to plug the hole. It was something he'd wanted to try for some time but had been afraid of rejection.

Pete started to squirm from side to side before thrusting against the pillow. "More."

Dylan reached for the ice. When he withdrew his fingers, water dripped out of Pete's hole. Without giving Pete's ass a chance to warm up, Dylan gently inserted two more cubes. Pete's moan was all the answer Dylan needed to push even farther. He landed a hard slap to Pete's ass, hoping the combination of pleasure and pain would set Pete off again.

"Fuck me," Pete growled in a voice Dylan hadn't heard before.

Dylan got to his knees and removed his fingers from Pete's hole before thrusting his cock inside. The shock of the cold flesh meeting the sensitive head of his cock almost took his breath away. "Jesus Christ," he gasped.

Pete didn't give Dylan a chance to move, instead he began fucking himself, moving back and forth against Dylan's dick.

It was the most erotic thing the two of them had tried, and it was fucking fantastic. Even better, Pete seemed to be enjoying it every bit as much as Dylan. It was an excellent sign of things to come.

Pete cried out his climax, but Dylan wasn't ready to give in yet. He gripped Pete's hips and took over, fucking as hard and fast as his body would allow. Each thrust warmed Pete's hole more and soon enough, Pete's body was as hot as it ever was. "Yeah, that's my baby," Dylan crooned. His need climbed higher and higher until he eventually gave in to his desire to come.

"Take it," Dylan said, grinding against Pete's ass as he came. He collapsed against Pete's back and closed his eyes. After catching his breath, he whispered, "Tell me I can stay."

A soft snore from the man under him was his only reply.

Chapter Seven

Pete knocked on John's office door. "Hey, you got a minute?"

"Sure, come on in."

Instead of sitting in one of the chairs in front of John's desk, Pete opted for the well-worn hunter green sofa. He'd given John a week to talk to Paula before scheduling the meeting. "How're things at home?"

John shrugged. "I took your advice and told her the truth."

"And?" Pete lifted his feet onto the coffee table and crossed them at the ankles.

"She kicked me out, said she didn't want me around the boys. I'm staying down the road at one of those cheapy motels until we can work out a settlement and get everything filed." John scratched his unshaven jaw. "It's for the best, I guess, but it's going to cost me. Things'll have to change around here."

Pete sat up. "She's going after the business?"

"Not the business itself, but half the equity, sure. If I know her, she'll probably try to keep me away from the boys. I'll fight her tooth and nail on that one, but I don't see any way out of the financial situation."

"I'm sorry, man." Pete wondered if John blamed him for Paula's reaction. John's sons were in high school and were currently working for the company. "Mark and Curtis won't let Paula keep them away from you. Those boys love you."

"Yeah, well, they loved the dad who was married to their mom. Neither of them have shown up for work since I left, so I guess they don't love me as much as you think they do." John jumped out of his chair and started pacing the office. "It's gonna kill me if I lose them and the business because I've decided to be honest with myself and my family after so many years of hiding that part of me."

"Have you thought of taking a partner?"

"I'm just feeling my way around this new lifestyle. I'm not near ready to get serious with anyone," John stated.

Pete chuckled. "I was talking about the business, not your sordid sex life, asshole. But since you brought it up, are you saying you've gone out with someone?"

"Are you trying to tell me you're interested in investing in the business?" John asked, ignoring Pete's question.

"I've been meaning to talk to you for a while about expanding Keep it Green to include landscape design and services. We both know I've got the capital, and I'd rather invest in something I love rather than stick it all in the bank." Pete held his breath. John's answer meant more to him than he'd realised.

"It would mean expanding the office or finding another building. I barely have room for the equipment I have now and this shithole is the only office in the place."

"I know. I've already gone online to see what kind of commercial properties are out there, and I found a couple that would work. I haven't contacted anyone about them or anything because I wanted to talk to you first."

John sat back in his chair. "We'd have to wait to make everything official until my divorce is final."

"We can do that. I'll use my money to start setting up the new building, so by the time you're free and clear, we can hit the ground running." Pete rubbed his hands together. It was only the second time since he'd inherited the fortune that he was grateful for it. The first being the decision to hire Dylan, of course.

"Just don't get carried away," John warned. "I've managed to run this company in the black for years. I don't like the thought of going into debt again."

"I'll cover the new building and anything that Paula gets in the divorce, in exchange for fifty per cent of the company," Pete offered.

John laughed. "I think you'd better talk to your lawyer first because you're coming out on the short end of that deal."

"I'll talk to Matthew, but he's not going to change my mind."

* * * *

"You're crazy," Matthew said. "There's no way you'll ever get that much money out of that company."

"Don't care," Pete replied. "If it helps, I plan to sell the mansion as soon as it's finished."

"Sure that'll help the bottom line, but it won't change the fact that you're about to dump a fortune into an investment that you can't recoup."

"Don't care," Pete repeated. "I'm never going to be the kind of person who goes out and buys a million dollar house or jets off to Europe for the holidays. My life's here, so if I want to make myself more comfortable by buying a slightly larger home and investing in a company I believe in, I'm good with that. It's a hell of a lot more than I had six months ago."

Matthew surprised Pete with a grin. "David warned me about you, but I thought he was full of shit when he said you wouldn't be comfortable with the money."

For some reason, the remark angered Pete. "David didn't know anything about me because he pushed me away when I was only nineteen years old."

Matthew shrugged. "I wasn't lying. David said almost those exact words to me. Funny, for someone who didn't know a damn thing about you, he pretty much hit the nail on the head, didn't he?"

* * * *

"John."

"Hey, is Pete in the office? I can't seem to reach him on his cell." Dylan grabbed his gym bag out of the passenger seat and headed across the parking lot.

"He's not here, but I think he had a meeting with his lawyer," John answered.

"Yeah, now that you say that, I do remember him mentioning it. Damn, I was hoping he'd work out with me over lunch. I've been working on the base of the living room fireplace all morning and have managed to kink up my back."

"Are you going to Brookside?" John asked.

"Yeah—why, you interested?" Dylan liked the idea of getting to know John better. From what Pete had told him, John was really having a rough time of it lately.

"If you don't mind? I called about joining, but the guy who answered the phone said there was a waiting list. You think they'd let me in as a guest of yours?"

"Absolutely, and I'm sure if we talk to Mike or Ray, they'll find you a spot if you're still interested." Dylan knew the waiting line wasn't as long as the staff led people to believe. It was all part of the club's marketing strategy.

"Yeah, I'd like that. I'll have to run by the hotel, but I'll call when I get there and you can meet me at the front desk."

"Sounds good." Dylan hung up and stuck the phone in his bag. "Hey."

"Hey, yourself," Josh greeted, leaning forward against the counter. "Here by yourself today?"

"For a while. I've got a friend coming in to meet me. Can you page me when he gets here? His name's John."

Josh licked his lips. "Is he hot?"

Dylan shook his head. He doubted there were many men in the club who Josh didn't find sexy. "Early forties, shaved head, brown eyes and several tattoos. Yeah, he's hot."

"I'll page you after I work some magic on him," Josh said, mischief in his voice.

Normally, Dylan would have warned Josh away, but he figured John might be interested in the skinny twink. "Go for it."

"Thanks."

Dylan entered the locker room and headed for his usual spot. He took off his T-shirt as a familiar sound caught his attention. When he'd come clean to Pete about listening to Manny fuck a guy in the shower,

Pete had shaken his head and had rolled his eyes. "No touching," Pete had ordered.

Dylan had no intention of touching anyone except Pete, but he couldn't resist taking a peek. After he finished changing, Dylan walked over to the communal shower. As he expected, Manny had some guy bent over while he fucked the hell out of him.

"Hey," Dylan greeted his friend.

Without breaking his rhythm, Manny turned his head to smile at Dylan. "Hey, I didn't think you were coming in today."

"Had a change of plans. I'm meeting one of Pete's friends here to give him the tour."

The handsome stranger's head snapped around. "Pete?"

Manny gave the man a hard slap on the ass. "Shut up and take my cock."

Dylan's cock lengthened at the smack. *Shit.*

"This is Linc, Pete's ex," Manny introduced, delivering another blow to Linc's ass.

Dylan's cock deflated as he backed out of the shower, suddenly feeling sick to his stomach.

Manny laughed. "Wait for me. I'm almost finished."

"I'll be outside," Dylan called back. He left the locker room and headed straight for the treadmill. He'd finished a mile before Manny made an appearance.

"You mad at me?" Manny asked, pushing a button on Dylan's machine to increase the incline.

"No. You can fuck who you want as long as it's not me or Pete. Guess I was just surprised to meet Linc in there with you." Dylan jumped to the sides of the machine and shut it down. "I thought he was living with Ray's ex?"

"He is." Manny leaned his forearms on the railing. "Linc comes in every couple of weeks to get special attention." He smiled, flashing those incredibly white teeth of his. "What can I say? I'm good at what I do. Keeps 'em coming back for more."

Dylan stepped off the treadmill and wiped the sweat from his face. "I was thinking about introducing you to John, Pete's best friend, but I'm not so sure you're what he needs anymore."

"Why? What's wrong with me?" Manny asked, genuine hurt in his expression.

"John's just getting into the game. I thought for a minute that you'd make a good teacher, but I can't see him bending over in that shower."

"You'd be surprised." Manny winked.

"John's a good guy. He just needs someone to show him the ropes, not break his fucking heart."

"I don't do hearts," Manny clarified in case Dylan had forgotten.

"I know, but something keeps those men coming back, and I don't think it's entirely your cock."

Manny rubbed the front of his thin shorts, drawing Dylan's attention to the obvious outline of his oversized cock. "I would disagree with you on that, but I think you're right. I think it's human nature to crave what you can't fully have." He gave his cock a squeeze before releasing it. "I don't really give a shit why they bend over as long as they do."

Dylan gave Manny a shove. "Stop trying to sell me on the player bit, I'm not buying." He knew there was more to Manny than his looks or his dick. It wasn't always obvious, but they'd had some really good conversations over the months since they'd become friends. Manny was a lot deeper than anyone gave him credit for, anyone except Dylan.

Dylan's name was announced over the loudspeaker, cutting the conversation short.

"John's here. You want to come meet him, or are you going to continue to act like an asshole?"

In a rare move, Manny reached out and ran a hand over Dylan's closely cropped hair. "You see too much."

Dylan shook his head. "No I don't. I see what's real." He took off, leading the way down the steps. Even from their distant vantage point, it was easy to see that Josh was all but stripping his clothes off in an effort to get John's attention.

"God I want that little ass," Manny said, low enough that Dylan barely heard him.

"Josh's?" Dylan asked, waiting for Manny at the bottom.

"Yeah."

"I'm sure he'd be more than happy to oblige," Dylan pointed out.

"Nope, I've tried time and time again and that fish ain't biting." Manny sneaked behind the counter and pressed himself against Josh. "How's my favourite receptionist today?"

Josh pushed back in an effort to knock Manny away, but barely succeeded in budging the much bigger body. "I've told you, I'm not going to be one of your regulars, now back the fuck off," Josh ground out.

Damn. Dylan hadn't known Josh had that much fight in him. *Good for him.*

Dylan held out his hand to John. "Glad you made it."

* * * *

Dylan watched Manny closely as the trainer showed John how to use the different equipment. Either Manny wasn't attracted to John or he was afraid of Dylan's wrath because he hadn't made a single move on John and it had been thirty minutes.

Instead, John and Manny seemed to be getting along great despite the scene John had witnessed between Manny and Josh earlier. It had been obvious to Dylan that John had been uncomfortable at the exchange, but his discomfort hadn't lasted long once they'd reached the top of the stairs.

"So with the membership, I can come and go as much as I want, right?" John asked.

"Yep." Manny led them into the pool area. He acknowledged a few of the regulars as he led John and Dylan towards the VIP Wet Room. Manny leant down and scanned the badge that hung around his neck and the door unlocked. "This part of the club costs a few bucks extra each month, but it's well worth it."

"Shit," John said upon entering the room.

Dylan stared at the giant hot tub. Big enough to hold at least fifty people, the tub was one of the luxuries in the club that he and Pete hadn't tried, preferring to do their fucking in private.

There were three men in the water, openly touching each other while carrying on a conversation about the fiscal cliff.

"Is it always like this?" John asked.

"This is pretty tame, but it's only one in the afternoon. It really gets going around nine at night or eleven on the weekends," Manny explained. He gestured to the condom dispensers set around the room. "If you're going to come, whether in someone's hand, mouth or ass, you have to be covered. That's the number one rule of this room. The only other rule that's strictly enforced is consent between all parties involved."

John glanced at Dylan before returning his attention to the men in the water.

Dylan grinned at Manny. It was obvious that John was intrigued by what he saw going on in the hot tub. "You wanna stay a while? I can finish my workout and come back for you," Dylan offered.

John eventually tore his gaze away from the men. "No, that's okay, but I think I'll check out the VIP membership prices."

* * * *

"The floors are going in today," Dylan announced as he walked into the kitchen.

Pete pulled Dylan's head down for a deep kiss before handing him a cup of coffee. "John and I are supposed to meet that Realtor about the building in Overland Park this morning, but I can stop by after that."

Dylan was nearing the end of the job, and needed to talk to Pete about what came next, but he kept putting it off. With only the moulding he'd ordered left to put up, he'd be finished in the next two weeks, and that was if he stretched it out. "What time's your meeting?"

"Nine." Pete opened the morning paper and started looking through the classifieds. "What about you?"

"Around the same." Dylan carried his coffee over and joined Pete at the table. He tapped his fingers on the side of the cup, and tried to come up with a tactful way to start the discussion. "I should be finished in a couple weeks."

Pete jerked, spilling his coffee in the process. "Really?"

"Yeah." Dylan reached over to the counter and grabbed a towel.

"Then what?" Pete mopped up his mess. "Will you go back to Maine or stay here?"

"I guess that depends on you," Dylan replied.

Pete stood and carried the soaked towel to the sink. "I want you to stay, but I know that it's been hard for you to be away from Pops."

"I'll have to talk to Pops about it, but my heart's in Kansas City now." Dylan abandoned his coffee and moved to wrap his arms around Pete.

"Do you think Pops would move here?" Pete finished rinsing the dishtowel and laid it out to dry.

"No, he won't move that far away from Grandmom's grave, but that doesn't mean I can't visit him every other month or so." Dylan hated the thought of not being there to take care of his grandpop, but Pops had never liked being taken care of anyway.

"That sounds like a good plan to me, but I don't want to get my hopes up until you talk to him. So let's shelve this for now." Pete spun around in Dylan's arms to face him. "I love you."

"I love you, too."

"Since we're being so honest with each other, I have to tell you something else," Pete said.

Dylan's stomach clenched. "Okay."

"I'm going to put the mansion up for sale as soon as it's finished."

It wasn't a surprise to Dylan. Pete had damn near told him that from the beginning, and although Dylan hated that he wouldn't be around to enjoy all the hard work he'd done on the place, he understood why it was necessary. "I figured that. I think it's the right thing for you to do."

"I was worried that you'd be mad," Pete admitted.

Dylan bracketed Pete's face with his hands. "I think it's better that you hold the good memories in your heart rather than in that house."

Pete's tight brow softened. "Thank you for understanding."

"Don't thank me. I'm for whatever makes you happy." Dylan gave Pete another kiss. "We'd better get going before we're both late."

"Yeah," Pete agreed. "I'm going to bring some boxes over to the house later and start packing up the second floor."

"Okay."

* * * *

Pete and John struck out with the building in Overland Park. It had the office space they needed, but the actual lot was too small to store their equipment. "I did like the location," Pete said. "It seems all the money is moving south to Johnson County."

"I agree," John said from behind the wheel. "But I'm worried that we won't be able to find a place we can afford with the square footage we need."

Pete stared out of the window as they drove through an older area of Prairie Village, one of the many suburbs that surrounded Kansas City. A house up on the right caught his attention. "Hey, pull over up there by that For Sale sign."

"You're crazy." John slowed and stopped the truck. "Don't even think about it, the house's a piece of junk."

Paying no attention to John, Pete got out and walked up the sidewalk. The yard and bushes were incredibly overgrown and the bottom step of the deep front porch had definitely seen better days. Old notices in the front window clued Pete in on how long the house had been sitting vacant. "I want this house."

Chapter Eight

Pete was so excited by the time John dropped him off at the mansion that he didn't even notice the floors in the foyer. He found Dylan in the kitchen eating a peanut butter and jelly sandwich at the counter. "I need you to come and look at something with me."

Dylan swallowed the rest of his sandwich, raised a finger for Pete to hold on a minute, and drank an entire glass of milk in one long gulp. "Something wrong with the floor?"

"The floor? No. Oh, hell, I forgot to look at it." Pete turned around and went back the way he'd come. The dining room hadn't been touched and the living room barely started, but the foyer was finished except another light sanding and the stain Pete had chosen. "Looks nice. They're doing a good job."

"They'll be back tomorrow morning to finish it. One of the guys had to take off the rest of the day to drive his pregnant wife to her sonogram." Dylan took a bite of another sandwich. "So what did you want to show me?"

"A house. I saw it on the way here. I called the Realtor we're working with for the new building and she said she'd call the listing agent and meet us over there." Pete couldn't stand still. He didn't know why the house had called to him like it had and John thought he'd completely gone off the deep end, but Pete felt like a kid on Christmas morning. "Please?"

Dylan finished off his sandwich in two bites. "Give me five minutes, and I'll meet you in the truck."

Pete launched himself at Dylan. "Thank you." He peppered kisses on Dylan's lips, chin and neck.

"Yeah, well, when my boss finds out I'm playing hooky, you can be the one to get my ass out of the fire."

Pete used the time to put Julie on her leash and take her out to pee. "The other house has a fenced back yard, so you can take all the time in the world to potty if you want, but for now, you need to hurry it up."

"I don't think she understands you," Dylan said from the doorway.

"Maybe not the words, but she gets the urgency in my voice," Pete corrected.

A few minutes later, Julie was back inside, and Pete was sitting next to Dylan in the truck. "Now, it needs some work, but the place could be absolutely amazing with a little TLC," Pete warned.

Dylan shut the gates as he pulled to the end of the drive. "Which way?"

"It's in Prairie Village."

Dylan patted Pete's leg. "Sorry, hon, but that means nothing to me."

"Sorry, take a right, go down to Seventy-Fifth Street and take another right." Although Prairie Village wasn't far, Pete realised he and Dylan had done little driving outside their regular routes.

Dylan rubbed Pete's leg. "I found something today while the guys were laying the floor."

"What's that?" Pete wondered if there was buried treasure under the old floorboards. Wouldn't that be a kick?

"I remembered what you said about packing up the second floor, so I decided to clean David's bedroom while I waited for you to get there," Dylan explained.

"And?" Pete glanced up at Dylan.

"I found a strongbox under David's bed. I'm not sure what's in it, but the lock looks fairly easy to break with the right tools."

Pete scratched the top of his head. "Has to be a gun or something, otherwise he would've put it in the safety deposit box at the bank."

"I left it on the bed."

"Thanks. We'll take it home with us when we go back to pick up Julie." Pete couldn't imagine his brother owning a gun, but after Pete had been kicked out of the house, he'd known little about David.

* * * *

Dylan's initial reaction to the place wasn't positive. "This it?"

"Yeah." Pete jumped out of the pickup and hurried over to a woman getting out of a silver sedan.

Dylan hung back, trying desperately to see what Pete saw in the place. He turned in a slow circle, checking out the other houses in the neighbourhood and liking what he saw until he faced the house that was for sale again. Was it the porch? Sure, it was the only one he could see that had a front porch, but that's all he saw.

"Come on," Pete called, walking up the path. "It's empty."

No shit, Dylan thought. He made his way to the porch and decided to bypass the steps altogether—safer, no doubt. He smiled at the confused-looking Realtor standing in the doorway. "Hi, I'm Dylan Oliver."

"Grace Beacham," she introduced herself, shaking his hand.

Dylan glanced over Grace's petite shoulder, looking for any sign of Pete. When he was satisfied the coast was clear, he leant down and softly asked, "How much?"

"Sixty-five. The bank believes the lot's worth that much," she answered, stepping back to allow Dylan entrance.

Dylan reached for a light switch.

Grace shook her head. "The electricity's been shut off for almost two years. No idea what the pipes are like after last winter, but again, the bank is selling it for the lot more than the house. It's a shame, really. I would imagine this is one of the oldest homes in this section of town."

It wasn't until Dylan managed to get the old roll blinds tucked up that he could see the interior for what it was. Graffiti covered the walls, like the house had been used as a party place or crack house at one point, but given the neighbourhood, he was betting on high-school kids with nothing better to do.

Heavy woodwork graced the living room although it had been covered with at least five coats of paint, the most recent a garish green. Still, the more he looked at the general layout and size of the rooms, he began to see hope for the old place.

"You've got to see the master bedroom," Pete said from the top of the staircase. "Come on."

Dylan stepped on the first tread and bounced, making sure the old wood would hold his weight. Not even a creak sounded. Impressive. He met Pete at the top of the stairs. "How many bedrooms up here?"

"Four, but I think there should only be three," Pete said. He grabbed Dylan's hand and pulled him into the first room. Huge windows looked out onto the back yard, but the most impressive thing about the room was the fireplace. "Isn't it fantastic?"

"Nice," Dylan agreed, a little less optimistic than his partner. He opened a door, hoping to find an en suite but seeing a small closet instead. "No bathroom."

"No, but that's where my plan comes in." Pete ran his hand over the wall. "On the other side of this is one of the smaller bedrooms, and on the other side of that is the bathroom for this floor. So I was thinking, why don't we tear that next room out and just make it a big master bath and walk-in closet. That would still leave us another two bedrooms, so plenty of room if Pops decides to visit or move in with us."

Dylan's heart melted. In all Pete's excitement over the house, he'd still included Pops in his plans. Dylan decided right then and there that he didn't care what the house looked like—if Pete wanted it, then that was good enough for him. "I think we should put an offer in on it."

"Offer, hell. I think I should write the bank a cheque tonight for the asking price," Pete countered.

As much as he wanted to argue, Dylan couldn't. Pete could have damn near any house in the city. The fact that he had his dreams set on a sixty-five thousand dollar house that needed a shit ton of rehab said more about the man he was than anything else. "Yeah, go for it."

"Really? You'll help me fix it up?" Pete asked, pure joy in his eyes.

"Absolutely."

* * * *

While Pete was on the phone with Matthew, Dylan decided to make the call he'd dreaded all day. After his conversation with Pete that morning about staying in Kansas City, Dylan knew he'd have to call Pops.

"Hello?"

"Hey, Pops."

"You're late today," Pops said. "Everything okay?"

"Yeah." Dylan paused while he gathered his words. He eventually decided to just come out with it. "Pete wants me to stay in Kansas City after the job's done."

Another pause, this time from the other end of the phone. "And is that what you want?"

Although Dylan had hinted to Pops about his growing feelings for Pete, he hadn't actually come out and said it. "I love him, Pops."

"Mmm hmm, I had a feeling that was the case. I've never known you to take so long on a single job."

"It was a really big job," Dylan said, defending himself.

"Yeah, I can tell by the pictures you sent, but I've worked with you all your life, and I know you should've had that one done a couple months ago."

Dylan felt like he'd just been chastised for goofing off. "Are you mad?"

Pops chuckled. "What right would I have to be mad? Live your life, boy. I've already lived most of mine. I wouldn't give up a minute of the time I got to spend with my Janet. I hope someday you feel the same about Pete."

"I think I already do. When Grandmom was alive, I couldn't understand why you never wanted to take those high-paying jobs out of state, but I do now."

"Does that mean you're sticking close to home from now on? Is there enough work for you to do there?" Pops asked.

"I hope so. If not, I guess I'll just go to work for Pete cutting grass and planting trees." Dylan didn't think he'd have a hard time picking up projects in the area, but he was willing to do whatever it took to stay with Pete.

"Nothing wrong with hard work."

"You're right. We're also buying a house that needs a ton of hard work, but Pete's so taken with the darn thing that I couldn't say no," Dylan admitted.

Pops chuckled again. "I know that's right. Who do you think picked out this place? Your Grandmom never asked for much, but when she wanted something, I learned it was best to give it to her. Else wise, I'd be sleeping on the couch."

Dylan smiled. He liked the happiness he heard in his grandpop's voice. "I love you, Pops. Thanks for everything you've done for me. I know you and Grandmom didn't have to take me in like you did, and I know I don't say it enough, but I appreciate it."

"One look at those big brown eyes and you captured our hearts. You're our blood, son, don't forget that we love you."

Although Pops had always taken care of Dylan like he was his own son, he'd never verbally expressed his love for Dylan in the way he just had. "I appreciate that. Promise that you'll come and see the house once we get it finished? Pete would love it if you'd stay for a while."

"We'll have to see how long it takes you. I'm not getting any younger, you know."

It was a typical answer from Pops, but one Dylan could live with. "Okay, I'll check again once it's done."

* * * *

"Hey," Dylan said, coming into the living room to join Pete on the couch. "How's it going?"

"Tough," Pete said, covering his face with the letter David had left for him in the strongbox along with several pictures of the two of them as kids, a few of the medals Pete had won in track and a birthday card for every year they'd been apart. It was like David had locked Pete away in a box to keep him safe from their father. All Pete could do was speculate because David didn't explain in the letter why he'd had a box of Pete memories under his bed.

Of course as he was taking the emotional trip down Memory Lane, he hadn't known Dylan would walk in on him acting like a fucking baby, but it was too late. He was sure Dylan had already seen the tears and snotty nose.

"Are you finding any answers at least?" Dylan asked, moving to get Pete a tissue.

"Some. I'm getting answers to questions I didn't even have, and little on the questions I do," Pete admitted.

"Like?"

"How much David hated the mansion. And Dad," Pete added. "He apologised for being weak when he was younger, but said he didn't know how to bridge the gap of what had happened between us once Dad was gone."

"Did he tell you why he trashed the house?" Dylan asked, enfolding Pete in his arms.

Pete nodded. "According to Dad's will, David wasn't allowed to sell it. I guess David thought of it as Dad's last act of control over his life. He didn't come out and say it, but I get the feeling that's why he did what he did."

Pete took a deep breath. "The really stupid part is that I like the man who wrote this letter." He wiped his nose. "David said he didn't know why Dad reacted the way he did after Mom died, but he'd heard rumours that some guy came up to him at Mom's funeral, claiming he was my father."

"You think he was telling the truth?" Dylan asked.

"Don't know, but Dad evidently believed him without bothering to check the facts because the next thing I know I was disowned. He never seemed to like me anyway. Maybe he'd suspected all along that I wasn't his." It was a hard thing to wrap his mind around, and Pete figured he'd probably wonder for the rest of his life who he really belonged to biologically, but even if he knew the truth, it wouldn't change the man he'd become. The truth was he belonged to Dylan, Mike, Ray and John. They were his family as far as he was concerned.

* * * *

Pete adjusted one of the throw pillows moments before Dylan walked into the house with his grandpop in tow.

"Here we are, home sweet home," Dylan announced.

A much older version of Dylan walked into the house, wearing knit pants, a white dress shirt and a silver and turquoise bolo tie. Pete stepped forward and held out his hand. "It's so good to have you here," he greeted.

Pops stared at Pete's hand for a moment before pushing it aside and wrapping Pete up in a big bear hug. "Families hug, strangers shake."

Pearls of wisdom, as Dylan called them. "Yes, sir." Pete hugged back.

"Pops," the old man corrected.

"Pops," Pete echoed, taking a step back.

"Woowee, will you lookee there," Pops said, moving towards the fireplace. "I'd know that work anywhere." He turned back to Dylan. "Nice job. Couldn't have done it better myself."

"That's high praise coming from you," Dylan said.

Pops moved closer to the fireplace and spent a few moments inspecting the intricate details of the carvings, nodding his head in approval as he did. "You should be proud of yourself, son."

"I am," Dylan stated. "The new owners of the Braxton Mansion contacted one of the local decorating magazines about the work I did. So the magazine came by and did a story on me for one of their upcoming issues. Hopefully, once people see my work, I'll be able to get a few more jobs."

"They'll be lining up around the block." Pops shook a gnarled finger at Dylan. "Mark my words. You'll be so busy you'll have to turn jobs away."

"I hope so."

"Are you hungry?" Pete asked. "Dylan said you liked chilli, so I made a big pot."

"I'd like to wash up some first. No sense in spreading all those germs from the plane around your nice house."

Dylan picked up the suitcase. "I'll show you to your room. There's a bathroom next door to it."

"Sounds good."

Pete watched the two men climb the steps. He couldn't believe how much Dylan looked like Pops. It was like looking fifty years into their future. The thought of Dylan still climbing those same stairs for the next fifty years brought a smile to Pete's face.

Yeah, he could handle that.

About the Author

An avid reader for years, one day Carol Lynne decided to write her own brand of erotic romance. Carol juggles between being a full-time mother and a full-time writer. These days, you can usually find Carol either cleaning jelly out of the carpet or nestled in her favourite chair writing steamy love scenes.

Carol Lynne loves to hear from readers. You can find her contact information, website details and author profile page at http://www.total-e-bound.com.

Total-E-Bound Publishing

www.total-e-bound.com

Take a look at our exciting range of literagasmic™
erotic romance titles and discover pure quality
at Total-E-Bound.